HYSTERIA

AN ALEXANDER GREGORY THRILLER

LJ ROSS

ISBN: 978-1-912310-52-4

First published in 2019 by Dark Skies Publishing

Author photo by Gareth Iwan Jones

Cover design by Stuart Bache

Cover design copyright © LJ Ross

OTHER BOOKS BY LJ ROSS:

THE ALEXANDER GREGORY THRILLERS IN ORDER:

1. Impostor

2. Hysteria

3. Bedlam

THE DCI RYAN MYSTERIES IN ORDER:

1. Holy Island

2. Sycamore Gap

3. Heavenfield

4. Angel

5. High Force

6. Cragside

7. Dark Skies

8. Seven Bridges

9. The Hermitage

10. Longstone

11. The Infirmary (prequel)

12. The Moor

13. Penshaw

14. Borderlands

15. Ryan's Christmas

"No one who, like me, conjures up the most evil of those half-tamed demons that inhabit the human breast, and seeks to wrestle with them, can expect to come through the struggle unscathed."

—Sigmund Freud, Dora: *An Analysis of a Case of Hysteria*

PROLOGUE

Jardin des Tuileries, Paris
September 2019

There were worse places to be than Paris in the autumn.

The city was resplendent in the early morning sunshine, which touched the rooftop of the Palais Garnier with trailing fingers and burnished the River Seine a rippling, molten gold. There, the Old World reigned supreme; its gentle arches and Lutetian limestone the stuff of lovers, artists, writers and—of course—the very rich.

But wherever you went, the gutters still stank of piss.

Eva Bisset hardly noticed its stench as she guided her rickety scooter through the back streets of the 1st Arrondissement with the kind of blithe disregard for life, limb and traffic codes that came from knowing every corner and cobbled stone in that great city. Regal buildings passed by in a blur as she joined the bustling melee of drivers delivering food and flowers to the upper echelons of Parisian society, whose number had swelled in the weeks leading up to

1

Fashion Week—a bi-annual event that attracted celebrities, designers and models from around the globe, all of whom came to see and be seen.

Eva saw them.

She saw tall, glossy men and women posing outside the *Pyramide* of the Louvre or draping themselves over one of the picturesque wooden benches lining the banks of the river, dressed in scraps of geometric material that probably cost more than her apartment. She watched them from the shadows—invisible, unseen—and delivered gluten-free sushi to the waifs who dared to nibble on it, all the time wondering how wealthy you needed to be, or how unhappy, to refuse the offer of food even when you were hungry.

"Eh! Salope! Regarde óu tu vas, idiote!"

She swerved suddenly to dodge the bonnet of a taxi, ignoring a stream of abuse from its driver before hurrying onward, crossing an invisible boundary between the real world and one inhabited by a chosen few, whose whims and wants she catered to. She tried to imagine what it would be like, never having to worry about money or the lack thereof; to dine at the finest restaurants and sleep soundly every night, without fear.

But there were many kinds of fear, and Eva found herself wondering whether it was she who was the lucky one, for there were some who could stay in that glittering paradise but could never leave.

Orange and pink would be in fashion, next season.

A cursory glance towards the collection of people gathered around a fountain in the Jardin des Tuileries was enough to confirm it, and Eva raised an eyebrow at the garish display of silks billowing on the morning breeze. Painting a smile on her face, she hitched a large bag of insulated food over her shoulder and crossed the ground to meet them, panting slightly beneath its weight.

The garden was located in the centre of town, between the Louvre to the east and the Place de la Concorde to the west. Originally, it had been created by Catherine de Medici for the Tuileries Palace, and became a public garden following the Revolution. Nowadays, it was a place where tourists, students and Parisian yuppies could cycle, stroll and mingle or—in this case—gather to photograph the world's most beautiful men and women, wearing clothes that were more like works of art than apparel.

As she drew nearer, Eva paused to check the name on the delivery note.

Gabrielle Leroux.

Anybody who'd ever read a magazine in the hairdressers or at the beauty salon would recognise the name, and the woman it belonged to, but Eva had little time to read. Consequently, the name 'Leroux' meant very little to her, and she cast her eyes over the assembled crowd hoping for divine inspiration, which came in the form of a tall, burly man dressed entirely in black.

"Excusez-moi? Gabrielle Leroux?"

The security guard made a leisurely survey of her face, lingered for a moment on her chest, then jutted his chin towards a small white tent.

"*Elle est dans la tente,*" he muttered. "*Tu n'as pas un petit quelque chose pour moi?*"

She ignored the last part and brushed past him, perspiring heavily as steam rose up from the bag.

"*Puis-je vous aider?*"

A reed-thin woman with cold blue eyes scanned her body and then folded her arms.

"*J'ai une livraison pour Mme. Leroux?*"

The woman held out a hand. "*Je vais le prendre.*"

Eva held onto the bag and shuffled her feet. "*Ah, c'est cent soixante-dix euros...*"

The woman rolled her eyes and muttered something about not carrying cash, before dipping back inside the tent. Eva waited, staring hard at the ground as their conversation trickled through the gaps in the tarpaulin and turned her skin red with anger and shame.

Presently, the woman returned.

"*Voila,*" she said, and slapped a small wad of notes into Eva's hand—enough to cover the bill but nothing more.

Eva studied the woman's face for a long, uncomfortable moment, then murmured her thanks and beat a hasty retreat across the park.

Eva's own corner of the universe was vastly less glamorous than the one she left behind at the Jardin des Tuileries. The Barbès district was located in the north of the city, to the east of the more popular areas of Montmartre and Pigalle, where tourists flocked to see the mighty Sacré-Coeur and its panoramic views of the city, or the bright lights of the Moulin Rouge. Consequently, it was not yet gentrified and had few chain stores or homogenous coffee houses. Instead, it remained a vibrant, multi-cultural place where the air was infused with a mix of spices wafting up from the many restaurants and delis lining the Boulevard Barbès. Café Michel was one such place; a tiny bolthole tucked away from the main road, specialising in fancy world cuisine that catered to even the most delicate of palates. Eva's father had been the eponymous 'Michel', whose canny eye for business had enabled his restaurant to survive in an already overcrowded marketplace, before his untimely death robbed him of the opportunity to reap any of the rewards.

Her husband had taken over the running of the place.

At the thought of Jean-Pierre, a tiny shiver of fear ran up her spine, and she paused before turning off the scooter's engine, her fingers still gripping the ignition key.

What mood would she find him in today?

Usually, a bad day was followed by one or two good ones, whilst he was racked with guilt for whichever bruise or cut he happened to have bestowed the day before. Jean-Pierre could be charming then; solicitous and tender, like the first time they'd met. He would tell her how much he loved her, taking care to remind her that only *she* had the power to make him lose his temper. If he didn't care so much, if she didn't arouse such feelings of passion, he wouldn't be forced to lash out with a slap or a kick.

Or a fist to the face.

Eva's fingers strayed up to her right temple, where a tiny scar was all that remained from that particular episode.

It had been her fault, really.

She shouldn't have suggested that he was responsible for their apparent infertility. She should never have questioned his manhood, or suggested he go to the clinic to have a check-up.

A man had his pride, as he'd forcibly reminded her.

Her stomach gave a lurch as she thought of the baby now growing inside her. She should tell him—Jean-Pierre would be ecstatic, especially if it was a boy, and maybe it would bring out a softer side to his nature.

Maybe it would give her some respite.

She rested a hand on her womb and tried to imagine the tiny life growing inside her. It had only been a few weeks and she worried that, if she told her husband now, he'd blame her if she miscarried again. Jean-Pierre was a man of business, he liked to tell her, not a midwife. He didn't concern himself with women's troubles.

She closed her eyes and imagined downy hair and chubby cheeks; tiny fingers and toes.

A beautiful smile spread across her face, and she knew she could withstand whatever awaited her inside the Café Michel, because she was no longer alone.

CHAPTER 1

Hôtel Violette, Paris
Monday 23rd September
Paris Fashion Week

"Are you awake?"

Tom Fiddeman trailed a finger along his wife's spine, admiring its creamy texture, then edged a little closer across the bed.

"Hey," he whispered. "I said, are you—?"

Diane rolled over, swatting his hand away in the process.

"Yes!" she snapped. "I'm awake!"

Yawning widely, she focused on his face, which wore a smug, 'come hither' expression she recognised only too well after twenty years of marriage.

"Where's all this energy coming from, anyway?" she hissed. "Earlier on, you said you were too tired to walk around the Louvre, but you seem to have made a *miraculous* recovery."

"It's all thanks to you, *ma cherie*," he crooned. "We're in the City of Lovers…"

Diane snorted eloquently.

"Lord knows why I've put up with you all these years," she said, but her fingers reached up to brush his stubbled chin. "Waking me up at all hours of the night."

"It's only"—he craned his neck around to check the time on the bedside table—"ten past three."

She groaned. "I'll be fit for nothing, tomorrow."

"I like a challenge," he said, and wiggled his eyebrows to make her laugh.

"Well, since I'm wide awake…" she murmured.

Tom needed no further bidding and reached out to take her in his arms.

"*Wait!*" she said, a moment or two later. "Did you hear that?"

Tom could hear nothing but the rush of blood as it drained from the part of his brain that usually dealt with things like speech.

"I didn't hear anything…"

His voice was muffled against the side of her neck.

"I mean it!"

With a stifled groan, he raised his head and was about to repeat his previous denial when there came several loud crashes, followed by a blood-curdling scream.

"*Bloody hell,*" he muttered, scrambling off the bed. "Put—put a call through to the reception desk, love, while I go and see what's happening."

"Be careful!" Diane said, clutching a hand to her throat.
Another crash followed by a heavy thud.

Tom grabbed the first thing to hand, which happened to be a marble paperweight from the small bureau desk, and reached for the door handle.

Before opening it, he turned back to his wife and met her eyes across the room.

"Lock the door behind me."

When Tom stepped out into the long, dimly-lit corridor, he found two women huddled outside a doorway opposite his own, banging on the painted wood. If he hadn't been wildly in love with his wife, he might have remarked that they were two of the most beautiful women he'd ever seen—one blonde, one redhead, and wearing little more than wispy scraps of silk which he decided must pass for pyjamas in Paris.

"*Dieu merci!*" one of them cried, when she spotted him. "*Aidez-nous, notre amie est dans la pièce—*"

An expression of panic flitted across his face, and he set the paperweight back down on the carpeted floor.

"Er, *je ne*…speak French," he finished, lamely.

"English?" she replied. "I should have guessed."

She cast a meaningful eye over his cotton boxers, and the pasty legs beneath them, then gestured towards the door.

"Our friend is trapped inside," she explained, in worried tones. "We heard noises…please, help us—she might be hurt."

"My wife's calling reception now," he said. "What's your friend's name?"

"Camille," the other woman answered.

Tom stepped forward and raised a fist to bang on the door again, then tried the handle—but it wouldn't budge.

"Camille!" he bellowed. "Camille, open the door!"

He decided to try brute force, and threw his body against the wood, which didn't move an inch. Behind him, Diane stuck her head outside their bedroom door.

"Tom? What's going on? Are you—?"

Her eyes widened at the sight of her husband standing between two real-life French goddesses, and she pursed her lips.

"I was going to ask if you're alright, but it looks like you're doing just fine."

Before he could respond, there came the sound of footsteps approaching.

"*Que s'est il passé*? What's happened?"

The night manager arrived at a run, his smart emerald brocade uniform rumpled from the nap he'd recently been taking in his office downstairs.

There followed a stream of fast-flowing French from the two young women, before the manager—whose name turned out to be Alain Nehmé—shouldered them aside, called out a brief warning to the occupant of Number 30, and produced a universal key card.

The door opened with a quiet electronic buzz.

They spotted Camille Duquette immediately, lying face down on the Persian carpet at the foot of an enormous bed, her body slumped like a ragdoll. Thin trails of blood were spattered over the white bedspread, and gauzy curtains billowed on the cold breeze which blew through doors that had been left open to a small balcony outside.

"*Mon Dieu,*" Alain whispered.

"Well?" Diane Fiddeman demanded, from somewhere over his shoulder. "Aren't you going to check her? Call an ambulance, for God's sake!"

Spurred into action, the manager raised a hand in acknowledgement and forced himself to enter the room. He moved slowly, giving the body a wide berth—all the while dreading the prospect of finding a pair of glazed, dead eyes staring up at him.

"Mademoiselle?" he managed. "Mademoiselle Duquette?"

Alain reached for his mobile phone and used one hand to key in the number for the emergency services, eyes widening as he spotted more blood on the rug where Camille lay motionless. He trembled as he drew closer, and almost lost control of his stomach when he finally saw what had been done to a woman who had once been beautiful.

Camille's face was covered in blood, which seeped from a long, slashing cut running from her right temple all the way to her mouth. She wore a set of patterned silk pyjamas, which were in tatters from a series of wounds to her arms and torso, and her hand was outstretched, as if reaching out for help.

"*Quel genre d'animal ferait ça?*" he whispered.

In the corridor, the two young women stumbled away from the doorway and began to sob.

"There." Tom patted their shoulders awkwardly. "There, there."

When each girl clung to him, he sent his wife a very Gallic shrug, and hoped there wouldn't be repercussions later.

But Diane wasn't worried about that.

"Is she still alive?" she demanded of the manager.

Alain started to shake his head, then he noticed the shallow rise and fall of Camille's chest as she struggled to draw breath.

"*Oui!* Yes—she's alive!" he said, and shuffled ineffectually from one foot to the other.

Uncaring about crime scenes and preservation of evidence, Diane rushed forward and knelt beside the girl's body. Her heart wept at the sight of such devastation, and she immediately thought of her own two girls, at universities back in England. If anything should happen to them while she wasn't there, she hoped some other kind person would tend to their wounds, or hold their hands until somebody better qualified could do so. Out there in the darkness, another mother might be wondering and worrying about her daughter, who now lay crumpled on the floor—her body torn by the hand of a madman.

"What are you going to do?" the manager whispered.

Diane removed her dressing gown and draped it over the girl's shivering body.

"I'm going to stay with her," she said, quietly.

Without another word, she reached across to take Camille's cold, blood-stained hands in her own and began to rub them in gentle, soothing circles while she hummed an old lullaby she'd once sang to her own babies.

CHAPTER 2

Wednesday 25ᵗʰ September
Two days later

The Grand Salon of the Sorbonne University was an impressive space made up of centuries-old wooden panelling adorned with classical works of art. Over the years, it had played host to everything from academic ceremonies to weddings, but today it welcomed a large delegation of senior police detectives drawn from major cities around the world— as well as a number of eminent men and women in the field of clinical and forensic psychology—who had gathered for a conference on 'Criminal Profiling and the Police'.

Doctor Alexander Gregory stepped up to the lectern at the head of the room and swept his gaze over the assembly, sharp green eyes sizing up their body language before diving into the speech he had prepared on the Eurostar journey from London the previous day.

"I'd like to thank the *Officiers de la Police Judiciaire* for inviting my colleague, Professor William Douglas, and me, to speak here today," he began, with a nod for his friend who was seated on the front row having already delivered his speech. "Before going any further, I should tell you that it's thanks to his guidance and support that I was able to carve out my own career as a clinical psychologist at the Southmoor Psychiatric Hospital in London. He was the first person to spark my interest in the concept of 'criminal profiling', and our mutual desire to help the Major Investigation Team at the Metropolitan Police led us to establish a special department in that area."

Gregory paused, searching to find the right words to express his crushing disappointment when their department had been used as a scapegoat by the same people they'd tried to help.

But he didn't mention any of that.

"The question many of you may be longing to ask is, 'Does profiling really work?' "

He watched people sit up a little straighter in their seats.

"The answer is both 'yes' and 'no'," he said. "The success of criminal profiling in helping to bring about the correct resolution to a serious investigation such as rape or murder depends on three variables: the quality of the evidence gathered by the police; the quality of a profiler's abilities; and, most importantly, the quality of the ongoing conversation between the police and the profiler."

"What do you mean by 'conversation'?"

Gregory sought out the source of the interruption, and locked eyes with a short, heavy-set man somewhere in his late forties, seated near the back of the room.

"I mean simply an ongoing dialogue, where the police enable the profiler to form an educated view on their investigation by allowing him or her full access to their dossier, as well as the various lines of enquiry, without seeking to hold back pertinent facts. In return, the profiler should not seek to misinform the police or misinterpret the information, exclude relevant information to suit their working theory, nor betray the confidence the police have placed in them. A profiler should discuss the possible reasons behind a perpetrator's actions as fully as possible, based on their previous experience dealing with criminal behaviour, where patterns can often be studied empirically and applied to novel situations."

"You advocate a clinical approach, then, rather than an instinctive one?"

Gregory nodded.

"I am a clinician first and a profiler second," he said, and then gestured to the walls above their heads. "Hanging at either end of this room are two paintings by Benjamin Constant, both inspired by the Greek myth of Prometheus, the titan who defied the gods to champion mankind. One represents 'Prometheus Enchained', symbolising the past, and the other is 'Prometheus Unbound', symbolising the future. I suggest that we take our own inspiration from these paintings and use our scientific faculties to look to the future and to progress. Together, profiling and the police can be a force for good."

When Gregory exited the stage a short time later, it was to warm applause. After shaking a few hands and exchanging an obligatory word here and there, he made directly for the drinks reception, where his friend awaited him.

"You must be parched."

Bill Douglas held out a glass of something red and fruity, which Gregory proceeded to chug down in three large gulps.

"Thanks, I needed that."

Douglas tipped up his pinky finger and swirled his own glass of wine, making a show of sniffing its bouquet.

"This is a fine Bordeaux," he said, haughtily. "Not the kind of plonk you youngsters knock back on a Friday night."

Gregory merely smiled, struggling to remember the last time he'd been out on a Friday night, let alone 'young'. He might only be a man in his thirties, but his heart and mind felt decades older.

"Plonk or not, it hits the spot," he said cheerfully, and smiled at the waitress who offered him a refill. "Why not? I'm off the clock now."

"It's about time you let loose a bit," Douglas agreed, casting a surreptitious eye over his lean frame and shadowed eyes. "You've been distracted since that case in Ireland."

Gregory thought back to the previous month, when he'd been called in by the Garda of a small, rural town in County Mayo to help them catch a killer. It had been a draining experience but a rewarding one—if you counted the fact that a murderous spree had been cut short before any more lives were lost.

No, it wasn't that which kept him awake at night.

What then, Alex?

His mother's voice echoed around his mind, and he took another hasty gulp of wine as he tried to block it out.

Even in death, she continued to haunt him.

When he looked up again, he found his friend watching him closely. Bill Douglas was an imposing man of around fifty, whose taste in clothes tended towards academic eccentricity and blended perfectly with his surroundings at the University of Cambridge, where he now spent much of his time. He'd been more of a father than his own had ever been, and the burden of keeping secrets from him was becoming too great to bear.

Now seemed as good a time as any to purge himself.

"It isn't the Irish case," Alex said, and set his glass down. "I—look, Bill, there's something I've been meaning to talk to you about…"

Before he could finish the sentence, Gregory caught sight of a man approaching, and recognised him as being the one who had interrupted his speech earlier.

"Professor Douglas and Doctor Gregory?" he asked, without any preamble.

"Yes," Bill replied. "Can we help you?"

"I'm Mathis Durand, from the *Brigade Criminelle*," the man replied, and produced an identification card for inspection. "The Commissaire has requested your attendance at *le trente-six*."

The 'Thirty-Six' was a colloquial reference to the old headquarters of the *Direction Régionale de la Police Judiciaire de la Prefecture de Police de Paris*—the criminal police of Paris, commonly abbreviated to 'PJ'. Its former headquarters had been at 36 Quai des Orfèvres, an iconic address only a stone's throw from Notre-Dame cathedral and, whilst they had since moved to the Rue du Bastion, they'd chosen to take the number 'thirty-six' with them, in keeping with tradition.

"Would you come with me, please?"

Gregory and Douglas exchanged a meaningful glance, as nearby heads turned in curiosity.

"Are we under arrest?"

Douglas was only half joking. The Brigade Criminelle was an elite squad of the Police Judiciaire, dealing exclusively with the most serious offences, and was not to be taken lightly.

"This way, please."

"We're not going anywhere until you tell us what this is all about," Gregory said.

"Murder," Durand barked. "You want a conversation, *Docteur*? We have one for you."

CHAPTER 3

"The case concerns attempted murder, to be precise."

Commissaire Adrienne Caron was an impressive woman, not least because she was one of only a handful of female faces at the Trente-Six. Despite efforts to reduce gender disparity in their ranks, the Police Judiciaire remained a steadfastly male-dominated environment and, truth be told, it gave Caron a good deal of personal satisfaction to know that she'd risen to the top of the police hierarchy in spite of it. Now, she commanded several specialist teams, including those belonging to the Brigade Criminelle.

She was seated at the head of a small conference table at the new police headquarters, with a breath-taking view of the city at her back. Gregory and Douglas were at the opposite end, and the remaining occupants of the table consisted of Mathis Durand and two other middle-aged men. In contrast to the former's rumpled shirt and egg-stained tie, both were highly groomed, boasting expensive haircuts and even more expensive suits, which seemed an unlikely choice for the average bobby.

On the other hand, this was Paris, not London.

"Thank you for agreeing to meet with us, Professor Douglas, Doctor Gregory," the Commissaire said, in fluent English. "I believe you've already met Mathis Durand, who is leading the team of detectives in charge of the investigation— strictly, he is the *chef de groupe* with the rank of *Capitaine,* but we usually still call him by the old title of *Inspecteur.*

"Can't teach an old dog new tricks," the inspector said. "Isn't that what you say, in England?"

"Allow me also to introduce *Procureur* Raphael Segal, and *Juge* Felix Bernard."

Both nodded politely.

"You must excuse me," Douglas said. "But, in England, it isn't customary for a representative of the prosecution, or a judge, to attend meetings during an active investigation."

Caron nodded and leaned back in her chair.

"Here, we have a different system," she explained. "In England, you have the Crown Prosecution Service, who take the police case to trial only after an investigation is complete. In France, the role of 'procureur', or prosecutor, is different. The prosecutor is an officer of the State, who attends the crime scene in the early stages and is part of the team who investigate the crime."

She gestured to Segal.

"Procureur Segal attended the crime scene shortly after Mathis and the other responding officers, for instance."

Douglas nodded.

"As for *Juge* Bernard, his role is also different from that of an ordinary trial judge in England," she told them. "Here, a 'juge' is more like…ah, something of an examining magistrate, perhaps. It is Felix's job to supervise the work of the homicide team and to re-examine witness statements and so forth, to ensure everything is done in accordance with the proper procedures."

"I also authorise forensic work, warrants and so forth," Bernard put in, and Gregory noted the way Durand's back stiffened in the chair beside him.

Tension there, he thought.

"Ordinarily, the Brigade Criminelle does not concern itself with simple homicides, or attempts," Caron continued, taking a delicate sip from an espresso cup before setting it back on its saucer. "We deal only with the most serious cases of murder in the city. However, we have made an exception in this case."

"Why?" Gregory asked.

She smiled, appreciating his ability to come straight to the point.

"It's different this time because of the sensitivity of the case…and of who the victim is—or, rather, who she is *not*."

Gregory frowned at her choice of words, and Caron nodded towards Inspector Durand, who took his cue.

"In the early hours of Monday morning, the control centre took a call from the Hôtel Violette," he began, in slow but precise English. "It's a nice hotel, not far from the Jardins des Tuileries. Officers attended a scene on the third floor, where they found a young woman, Camille Duquette, had been viciously attacked."

"Face and body slashed…horrible," Segal intoned, with a sad shake of his head.

"She survived and was taken to hospital, where her wounds were treated," Durand continued. "We are awaiting the results from our forensic team, but there were no obvious traces left by the assailant, and the knife or other weapon has not been found."

Gregory recalled seeing an image of a beautiful young woman plastered on the broadsheets over the past couple of days, alongside a headline about a model having been attacked in one of the city's luxury hotels. They'd christened her 'Sleeping Beauty'.

"What about CCTV?" Douglas asked. "Any witnesses?"

"There was no CCTV on that floor of the hotel, nor in the service stairs, which is how we assume the assailant left," Durand replied. "There are witnesses who overheard the commotion during the attack, but they didn't see anybody fleeing down the corridor."

"Did you recover a mobile phone?" Gregory asked.

"No, but we know that she had one," Durand said. "Maison Leroux and a couple of the other models had a number for Camille, but, when we tried calling it, the number went straight to voicemail. My team have already contacted the phone companies to try to locate it and access her messages. Aside from that, we have no leads."

Gregory frowned again, thinking it was a little premature to declare they had no leads, especially since the forensic results had not been returned and their victim was still alive to tell the tale.

"What does the victim say about it?" he asked. "Has she been able to give you an account of what happened?"

The others looked amongst themselves.

"That's just it, Doctor," Segal said, leaning forward to rest his forearms on the conference table. "Camille Duquette hasn't spoken a word since she regained consciousness."

Douglas turned to his friend.

"A mute patient, eh? It isn't often we find one of those."

Gregory heard the cajoling note to his friend's voice, but he wasn't ready to commit to anything just yet.

"What else do you know about her?"

Durand licked his thumb and flicked through a sheaf of papers to find the one he was looking for, then read the summary contained there.

"Camille Duquette, aged nineteen," he said. "According to the hospital notes, she is sexually active, but there were no signs of sexual assault following the attack. No unusual tattoos…Her most recent occupation is listed as 'fashion model', which is corroborated by her employer, Maison Leroux. She was due to attend her first catwalk show for them on the Monday morning, following the attack. I'm sure you're both aware, this week is Fashion Week in Paris," he added.

"It's unlikely she will ever model again," Bernard interjected, with a sad shake of his head. "Such a shame."

He slid a couple of photographs across the table. The first one was clearly a publicity shot, taken of a slender, statuesque woman with long, dark hair and bright blue eyes who stared into the camera with one hip cocked at an angle, as was customary. Beneath it was another photograph, taken in the hospital sometime after her attack, and she was almost unrecognisable with her skin swollen by a long, grotesque laceration running down the right side of her face, held together by dark stitches.

Gregory sighed, and pushed the photographs away.

"I'm very sorry for Camille but, sadly, these things are not unusual—"

"There is something else," Durand interjected. "It's possible that Camille Duquette may not be her real name. We recovered an identity card and a single bank card from her hotel room, belonging to an account that was set up less than three weeks ago, but we can find no other official records or permanent residence. It's possible she may be underage or a runaway of some kind—"

"Or an illegal migrant," Caron put in. "It's a big problem for us."

Durand nodded.

"It means we're having trouble tracing any family or next of kin—or finding out anything useful about her life before she started working for Maison Leroux."

"Where is she now?" Gregory asked.

"At a safe house," Segal replied. "The Leroux family offered to pay for a private apartment and a nurse until she is well enough to move on, or until our investigations are complete, whichever comes first."

"The Leroux are a man and wife team," Caron explained. "Armand Leroux is the business head, while his wife is the creative mind. We understand they hired Camille for the duration of Fashion Week, as well as for a number of separate catalogue and magazine editorials. They felt it only right to take care of her, especially as we haven't been able to locate any next of kin."

"Very generous of them," Douglas remarked. If he thought there was another, more cynical motivation for removing the woman from the public eye at such a crucial moment for their business, he said nothing of it.

"What kind of psychiatric help is she receiving?" Gregory asked. "Has any specialist care been arranged to help her to overcome the trauma?"

"She sleeps a lot," Segal replied. "It's part of her physical recovery. But, yes, a psychiatrist visited her today, and has a scheduled appointment every morning until her speech returns."

If it returns, Gregory thought. Nothing was certain, when it came to matters of the mind.

"Until she speaks, we have only the information from the crime scene and a few witness statements, which isn't much," Segal said. "We need something to work with."

"How do you imagine we can help?" Douglas asked. "We profile criminals, but we can't wave a magic wand."

"It would be helpful to know what kind of personality would do such a thing," the prosecutor replied. "Her wounds...it was as though a wild animal had inflicted them. We need to know who would attack in such a way."

Gregory huffed out a laugh.

"Without any of her personal history, how can we be sure she doesn't have enemies?" he said. "The attack might have been a punishment or gang-related in some other way. Does she have any history of drug abuse?"

"There was nothing in her system when she was taken to hospital, and the witnesses we interviewed said she was clean," Durand replied, and then pulled a face. "On the other hand, it's unlikely they would be forthcoming, if they feared incriminating themselves. It isn't unheard of, within the fashion world..."

"So drug abuse remains a possibility," Gregory said, and guessed it was something the police tolerated, so long as things didn't get out of hand. "It may also have been a jealous lover or colleague, a stalker, somebody she rejected..."

"Alongside many other possibilities," Douglas agreed. "The manner of the attack was brutal and possibly vengeful but, without speaking to the victim, it would be impossible for either of us to produce a meaningful profile at this stage."

Caron nodded thoughtfully.

"And, if we make it possible for you to meet with Camille tomorrow, do you agree to stay and assist the investigation?"

"Regrettably, I'm due to fly to Boston on Friday morning and must return to London before then," Douglas said, then cast a sideways glance towards his friend. "How about you, Alex?"

Gregory's lips twisted into a reluctant smile. He couldn't deny his interest had been piqued by the case, as well as his compassion. For any person to be rendered mute by such severe trauma was a cause of great sadness, and he yearned to help her—not merely so she could confirm her identity to the police and help to find the person responsible, but before any temporary damage became permanent and she was consigned to a life of silence.

He thought of his commitments back at Southmoor Hospital, but he wasn't due back in his office until the following week, as Douglas was very well aware. He'd hoped to spend a few days exploring Paris after the conference, taking leisurely strolls around its parks and museums, and had booked a few days' leave.

Perhaps another time.

"Yes," he said eventually. "I'll try to help."

CHAPTER 4

Later, Gregory accompanied his friend to the Gare du Nord train station, where Bill Douglas was due to catch the six-thirty Eurostar back to London. The air was crisp as it whipped through the side streets and both men turned their collars up against the wind.

"What do you make of it all?" Douglas asked, as they wandered past the Pompidou Centre towards the 10th Arrondissement.

Gregory laughed and stuck his hands in his pockets.

"Which part?" he said. "The part where we were frog-marched to Police Headquarters by a bloke who looked a lot like Jean Reno's shorter, hairier brother—or the part about the impossibly beautiful model who can no longer speak? Because, as far as the first part goes, I've had warmer welcomes."

Douglas chuckled.

"His manner leaves something to be desired," he agreed, diplomatically. "All the same, it's an interesting case. Selective mutism is rare in adults, don't you think?"

Gregory stuck his hands in his pockets and side-stepped a man on a Segway, who appeared to have enjoyed a liquid lunch and was now veering all over the pavement.

"Selective mutism is certainly more common in children, but the causal factors are the same in adults," he said. "It's an extreme anxiety disorder, leading to a selective inability to vocalise in certain social settings, despite no physical impediment to the vocal cords. It can strike at any time, including after a severely traumatic experience."

"Are we sure she isn't suffering from aphasia?" Douglas wondered aloud, referring to the impairment of language skills following a brain injury. "That could also account for the lack of speech."

Gregory thought back to Camille's medical notes contained in the police file, a copy of which now rested inside the briefcase he carried.

"She suffered a blow to the side of her head. It's possible that was sufficient to cause the level of brain injury usually associated with a neurological loss of speech, but aphasia is far more common following a stroke. There was some swelling on her MRI scan, but nothing like the levels we'd normally see in aphasiac cases."

"Mmm," Douglas said, as they waited to cross the road. "And we don't know whether the person who's tending to her is a specialist when it comes to speech therapy?"

"The psychiatrist is a man by the name of Ernesto Gonzalez, originally from Brazil. I'll look him up this evening and see what I can find out," Gregory said, following his friend's train of thought. "But they haven't asked me to take over any part of her care, Bill. They've asked me to come on board as a profiler."

"Things can change," was all Douglas said.

Up ahead, the lights of the station glowed brightly against the darkening sky, and their footsteps slowed.

"I wonder if she was talkative before her attack," Gregory mused. "What I really need to find out is whether Camille *can't* speak or whether she *won't* speak. In cases of selective mutism, severe panic causes a kind of freeze in their brain, inhibiting speech. Usually, they're still able to talk amongst their most trusted friends or family."

"Which, in this case, we can't find," Douglas reminded him.

"Exactly, which doesn't help us one little bit. On the other hand, given what the police told us about her lack of official paperwork, it's possible she could be choosing not to talk for fear of reprisal."

They had reached the entrance of the station, and people milled around, scurrying back and forth as they went about the business of living.

"If anyone can bring her out of it, you can," Douglas said, giving him a bolstering slap on the back. "I'll be in Boston from tomorrow night, but I'll have my mobile with me, if you need to call."

He turned to leave, then swung back around again.

"Earlier, at the Sorbonne, you were about to tell me something," he said. "Was it important?"

Gregory glanced up at the large iron clock hanging from the rafters above their heads, and schooled his features into a neutral expression, hating himself more with every day the truth was left unsaid.

I went against every professional code and treated my own mother, before she died.

She never recognised me, not once.

If anybody knew, I'd be struck off.

"I can't remember," he said. "It mustn't have been important."

With a light shrug, Douglas disappeared into the crowd, leaving Gregory to stare at his retreating back as the distance between them grew even greater than before.

Alex took his time heading back to his hotel in St Germain-des-Prés, which was on the south side of the river in an area known as the Latin Quarter. It was a cool, thirty-minute walk from the Gare du Nord, but he welcomed the night air as it burned his cheeks, making him feel *alive*. There was no moon that night, but the city was illuminated by a thousand twinkling lights, guiding the way as he strolled along tree-lined avenues.

The journey took him past the medieval cathedral of Notre-Dame, which had recently been ravaged by a catastrophic fire that destroyed its spire and most of the roof, while the rest of the world watched in horror from their living room sofas. As Gregory paused to look up at its charred façade, he wondered why it was that people mourned beautiful things—and beautiful people—more than the average, everyday beings that accounted for most of the world's suffering.

Don't be a hypocrite, his mother's voice whispered in his ear. *You're one of them.*

Much as it troubled him to admit it, he supposed that was true. Despite the shadows of his childhood, Alexander Gregory was a tall, good-looking man who never needed to look far to find company if he sought it—which he rarely did. There had been no barriers to entering his chosen profession, and he knew that the skin he wore, and the bones that held it all in place, were considered attractive by some. It was an odd psychological quirk, proven time and again, that people ascribed positive characteristics to those they considered physically attractive; it was a form of wish fulfilment that had allowed many an attractive rapist and murderer to escape detection, because people simply couldn't believe that a person who seemed so appealing on the outside could be a festering mass of dark thoughts and deeds on the inside.

When he thought of his own life, he suspected there had been plenty of times when his outward appearance had oiled the wheels of fortune; countless tiny, seemingly insignificant moments that could have ended very differently, had he been a different man. It was impossible to know for certain, and his ego wanted to believe that his clinical skills alone would have elicited the same results, regardless of other factors weighing in his favour.

But the truth, he suspected, was somewhere in the middle.

With these sobering thoughts circling his mind, Gregory crossed over the river and paused for a moment to admire the blazing lights of the Eiffel Tower's hourly show, reflected in the inky-blue depths of the Seine. But after the lights faded to darkness, he turned away from the road leading to his hotel and found himself wandering through the myriad network of small alleyways that criss-crossed the Latin Quarter, with no particular route in mind.

He wasn't ready to be alone just yet, especially not with himself.

The neon sign read, 'JAZZ TONITE'.

The club was a tiny, nondescript affair, with a black-painted door. A couple stood outside, smoking and kissing intermittently, while a bouncer leaned back against the stone wall and played on his phone. Alex watched them from the other side of the street, undecided about whether to go inside, until the door opened and a brief snatch of music burst out into the night, tempting him to step into the road and out of his comfort zone.

The bouncer gave him a quick pat-down, then jerked his head towards the door.

"*Pas de photos*," was all he said, before returning to his phone.

When Alex pulled open the heavy black door, he found himself at the top of a narrow stairwell leading down to the basement level, punctuated by a series of red-tinted nautical lamps. He smiled, wondering what the Health and Safety Officer back at Southmoor Hospital would have said about it, then continued towards the sound rising up from the gloom.

When he reached the bottom of the stairs, he made his way through another doorway leading to the main bar area, which was much larger than he expected. It had formerly been a cellar of some description, and its stone ceilings were low and arched, like miniature versions of the catacombs that ran beneath the oldest parts of the city. There was a bar at one end and a small stage at the other, with room enough for a piano and two other people, at most. A number of scarred wooden bistro tables had been crammed into the remaining space, each occupied by two or three people whose faces were lit by a single flickering tea light. He watched their shoulders jiggle up and down in time to the pianist, who was trilling out his own jazz version of 'Johnny B. Goode'.

"Oui, monsieur?" said the barman.

Gregory ordered a beer and took it to the edge of the room, where he leaned against a wall and let the noise roll over him. He stayed like that for a while, content to nurse his beer and tap a finger in time to the beat, enjoying the novelty of being amongst people who were neither his patients nor his friends.

Friend, he amended.

To have friends, one must first seek them out and then strive to keep them. Unfortunately, life had taught him to be cautious; since being a small boy, he'd learned never to trust the words that people said, but to read the language of their bodies, which was usually a more reliable indicator of their true feelings.

He raised his hands to clap as the pianist took a bow.

"Et maintenant, mesdames et messieurs, je vous présente la belle Mademoiselle Margot…"

There was rapturous applause—apparently, Mademoiselle Margot was already known to the regulars—and Alex watched a woman step onto the stage. She wore a simple black dress and, when she turned to speak to the pianist, he saw that her long legs were encased in forties-style tights, the kind with the seams running up the back. Blonde hair shimmered like a halo around her pale face, which bore no make-up except a slash of red against her lips.

He couldn't take his eyes off her.

"Merci bien, mesdames et messieurs," she murmured into the microphone, and then switched to English for the benefit of any tourists and ex-pats. "I'm going to sing a little ditty to remind you of summer."

When she began the first husky, opening bars of 'Summertime', Alex felt his whole body react. Her voice seemed to soar, filling the room with a sound so deep, he might have drowned in it. He couldn't seem to move while his body remained taut and trembling, and his fingers gripped the bottle of beer as if it were a lifeline. It had been a long time—a *very* long time—since he'd experienced a physical reaction so strong, and his instinctive reaction was to abandon his beer and run.

Coward, a small voice whispered.

And so, he stayed, mesmerised by the woman and her voice.

Margot sang mostly with her eyes closed, but as the number drew to a close, they opened again to stare dreamily around the room. When they came to rest on him, he felt his skin prickle beneath the heat of her gaze, but he didn't look away.

He smiled from the shadows, and told himself that one more drink couldn't hurt.

It was after two by the time Margot's set finished.

Gregory sipped another beer while he listened to her move seamlessly through a repertoire of old and new classics in an easy, playful style that drew in the audience and made them feel instantly at home. It was a technique he tried to teach his more antisocial patients at Southmoor, but the art of relating to one's fellow beings remained elusive to many.

Himself included.

There was a difference between engaging with other people, and merely observing them. He knew almost all the accepted theories about how to form meaningful relationships; he could teach others and, from time to time, dabble a little in the pursuit. But, mostly, he held himself apart. As a skilled observer, it was easy to spot when a person was becoming too close, or too dependent, and he knew it was time to withdraw. *He could recognise the signs of physical attraction, too*, he thought, watching Margot thank the audience and set her microphone back in its holder with a lingering glance in his direction.

The question was what to do about it.

CHAPTER 5

Thursday 26ᵗʰ September

Gregory returned to his hotel room sometime after five, and gave up any prospect of sleep in favour of blasting his body with a cold shower—during which he sang a bastardised version of 'Summertime', badly out of key. He spent the remaining pre-dawn hours poring over the police file, memorising names and pertinent facts, writing notes and trying to recall previous cases involving a similar kind of violence.

The decision to use a knife in Camille Duquette's attack rather than other less personal methods was revealing. Statistically speaking, men were more likely to commit bloody crimes and didn't tend to shy away from getting their hands dirty. There were also far more reported cases of male stalkers than female, but he wondered privately whether that was more to do with men not wanting to report their experiences to the police. Men might be more likely to attack in such a way, but he'd treated several women during his time at Southmoor whose crimes had been enough to turn his blood cold. Either way, it was too early in the investigation and there were too many unanswered questions for him to form an educated view.

Camille's unique profession as a fashion model, and the fact that her face was now irrevocably scarred, also seemed highly significant. He would even go so far as to say *ritualised,* which opened up the field of enquiry even more. Whilst it was possible a man or woman had developed an unhealthy love obsession with the beautiful Camille Duquette—whether by chance, or design—and had been motivated to attack her through jealousy or rejection, it seemed equally possible that someone had resented her good fortune in being plucked from the many thousands of other young women who aspired to join the elite world of high fashion, and decided to rob her of the life she might otherwise have enjoyed.

Spite was as good a motive as any.

As he packed away the file and shrugged into a light woollen coat, Gregory found himself wondering how the assailant had gained entry to Camille's hotel room. There was no evidence of forced entry recorded in the file, which begged the question of whether her would-be attacker had managed to procure a key card to the room—which was not unheard of—or clamber up to the veranda windows from the courtyard, three storeys below. *Unless…*

Unless her attacker was already known to her.

There would be no need to plan an elaborate entry if

they could simply knock on her door—especially since there was no CCTV covering the corridor or service access stairs outside.

For the right person, it would be child's play.

"You look like ass, my friend."

These generous words were spoken by Mathis Durand, who greeted Gregory inside the reception foyer of the Hôtel Violette shortly before nine o'clock.

Gregory glanced at himself in one of the mirrored panels on the wall and was forced to admit that Durand was probably right.

"You're no oil painting yourself," he replied.

Durand patted his rounded belly.

"I try, *mon ami*, I try," he said, and gave the younger man a more thorough inspection before letting out a bawdy laugh. "Paris was good to you last night, *eh*?"

Gregory declined to answer, and turned his attention back to their surroundings instead. The hotel was a boutique sort of place; an old, classy establishment that had received an injection of funds sufficient to attract bright young things who liked Instagram-able backdrops with plenty of gilt and marble. The staff wore immaculate emerald green uniforms complete with tiny, gold-embroidered caps perched atop their heads and, perhaps most impressive of all, they wore them with a smile.

"Fancy place," he said.

Durand seemed unfazed, leading Gregory to assume that, once you'd seen one impressive feat of Parisian architecture, you'd probably seen them all.

"The others haven't arrived yet, but we can start making our way upstairs to see the room where it happened," he said, raising a hand to summon one of his underlings, who trotted across the foyer. The young man nodded vigorously at Durand's instruction to remain downstairs and direct any new arrivals up to the third floor.

"He seems eager to please," Gregory remarked, once they were inside the lift.

Durand let out a grunt.

"His father works for the Ministry of the Interior," he said, and left it at that.

Gregory decided he liked the surly, red-faced man, who carried a general air of cigar smoke and cynicism so potent, it put the average Brit to shame.

The doors swished open and they stepped out into a plush corridor with oak panelling and cream-painted walls, accented by a series of fleur-de-lis murals. They had come to the Hôtel Violette to attend a '*reconstitution*', which was a blow-by-blow reconstruction of the crime. In French law, it was a crucial part of the investigation, organised by the *juge* and intended to stress-test the facts. However, it was normally arranged once the police had a suspect in mind, and was usually attended by them *and* the victim—or the victim's family—which had the potential to be an emotional melting pot.

42

"The reconstitution is crucial to uncovering the truth," Durand said, as if he'd read Gregory's mind. "Normally, it occurs much later in the investigation."

Gregory remained circumspect. It was one thing to think that a system was unusual, it was another to say as much.

"You brought the reconstruction forward this time—may I ask why?"

Durand pulled a face and began walking along the corridor.

"Not me, *mon ami*. The powers above," he muttered. "The Commissaire has heard from the Leroux family, the Mayor, and everyone else who would rather not start a panic this week. Did you see the news? The press have already found out about Camille, and they're calling her attacker '*Le Boucher de Beauté*'."

"The…Butcher of Beauty?"

Durand gave a short nod.

"The fashion industry is a big part of our culture here—and big business, too. There are some who welcome publicity at any cost, while others seek to suppress horror stories like these. There is politics at play, as much as policing. Juge Bernard and Procureur Segal are of the view that, since the girl can't speak and no family have come forward to report her missing, it's best to bring forward the reconstruction and see if anything can be learned from it. That's the official reason, in any case."

Gregory thought of all the well-heeled international students who travelled to Paris to study or work, all the celebrities who patronised the hotels and restaurants…yes, he could see why any or all of those businesses wouldn't want to frighten them away.

And yet, a woman had suffered a brutal attack, and had no family to support her—even if she wanted to speak.

"Will Camille be joining us at the reconstruction?" he asked.

"No, she's still too unwell to travel," Durand replied.

Gregory was relieved to hear it; he was a proponent of 'flooding' treatment in cases of mild phobias, but he doubted anything would be gained by exposing an already traumatised individual to the scene, especially so soon after the event.

"She has her appointment with Doctor Gonzalez this morning," Durand continued. "You can meet with her later this afternoon, if you wish."

They rounded a corner and spotted another police officer guarding the room where Camille had been staying.

"Do you think there's much to be gained from a reconstruction, if you have no suspect?"

Durand glanced across at him, then away again.

"I do the bidding of my superiors," he muttered, leaving Gregory to make of that whatever he liked. "Did you read the file? Was there anything you didn't understand?"

The paperwork had, naturally, been written entirely in French. As it happened, Gregory spoke the language fluently thanks to some time spent at an international school in Geneva, but he found that conversations flowed more freely between his foreign counterparts when they thought their company couldn't understand what was being said.

"I managed," he said, cagily.

Durand nodded, and exchanged a few words with the police guard before pointing to the rooms adjoining Number 30.

"The witnesses were in numbers 29, 31 and 35, which is on the other side of the corridor. We asked them to wait inside the rooms they were occupying on the night of the incident, so we'll collect them in a moment."

Gregory thought of the sequence of events, according to what they knew so far.

"The women resident on either side of Camille were both models employed by Leroux. Is that correct?"

Durand nodded, and spoke in an undertone.

"Like Camille, they were both on the roster to appear at a show on the day of the incident," he said. "In Number 29, we had Juliette Deschamps. She's twenty-two, and a *redhead*," he added, with a knowing look that entirely missed its mark.

"And in Number 31?"

"Madeleine Paquet, who is twenty-six, and blonde," Durand felt compelled to tell him. "Both women say they've only known Camille for ten days, after being introduced to one another at a party thrown by Leroux."

Gregory nodded.

"There wasn't much in their statements concerning their relationship with Camille, or any opinions about her character," he remarked. "Do you think they didn't get on?"

"Who can tell?" Durand said. "They may not have known her very well and, in fashion, it's a cut-throat world…no pun intended. It's possible they saw one another as professional rivals."

"Are both women resident in Paris?"

Durand nodded.

"Both have apartments in the city."

"Why stay at the hotel, then?"

"It was at the behest of Leroux," Durand replied. "They wanted everybody in one place, and it's near the venue where the show was to be held, in the Jardin des Tuileries."

Gregory nodded, wandering to the other end of the corridor to get the lay of the land, as well as to check for any other access points.

"Juliette says she heard a loud crash followed by a scream which woke her up, and she ran outside into the corridor to see what it was," Durand continued. "There, she found Madeleine already outside, banging on the door to Camille's room. She says she joined her and, shortly afterwards, an English man and his wife came from Number 35 to help."

"Tom and Diane Fiddeman?"

Durand nodded.

"Does Madeleine's account of the night's events match Juliette's?"

Durand pulled another one of his expressive faces and made the 'so-so' motion with his hand.

"According to Mlle Paquet, she came out of her room at the same time as Mlle Deschamps, rather than being the first to respond," he said. "A minor inconsistency, but…"

"Worth bearing in mind?"

"*Exactement*. As for the English couple, they are staying in Paris for a few days to celebrate a wedding anniversary. The man says he came from his room at around quarter past three in the morning, to find Juliette and Madeleine already in the corridor calling out to Camille and banging on the door."

Gregory recalled seeing a list of ten female and four male models working for Maison Leroux, all of whom were staying at the hotel on the night of the incident, presumably at the expense of their employer.

"Do you have statements from all the models in the hotel?" he wondered, not having seen a full complement. "Were any of them staying on this corridor?"

"The others had rooms on the first floor," Durand explained. "None recalled seeing or hearing anything. The other rooms on this floor were occupied by tourists, some of whom were not in the hotel at the time, others remained asleep until the arrival of the ambulance and the police. We gave them permission to leave, and we have their details if necessary."

Before Gregory could press him further, they spotted the juge and procureur rounding the corner, with the night manager Alain Nehmé in tow.

"Almost time to begin," Mathis declared, and raised a fist to knock on the first door.

CHAPTER 6

For the second time in the space of twenty-four hours, Alexander Gregory found himself staring into the face of an angel—one who happened to moonlight as a jazz singer when she wasn't showcasing high-end clothing for couture fashion houses.

"*Margot*?" he blurted out.

"Madeleine," she corrected him, with a meaningful glance towards the stocky inspector, who was watching their exchange with avid interest.

It didn't take long for Alex to join the dots, but it made for a very awkward picture all the same. The odds were incredibly long that, of all the people in Paris, a material witness to a crime and the police profiler should happen to meet one another. Apparently, he wasn't the only one to note the coincidence, because he sensed growing suspicion from Madeleine who was, no doubt, wondering how he had come to be there.

He wanted to remove that seed of doubt, but Gregory's first duty was to confess the nature of their relationship to the police and thereby remove any suggestion of bias in his dealings with their investigation. However, before he had a chance to explain, they were joined by the other parties to the reconstruction.

"Mlle Paquet?"

Procureur Segal wasted no time introducing himself, which he did with a flourish before moving on to the next young woman he felt worthy of his immediate attention.

Juliette Deschamps wore a bored expression and a pair of skin-tight, leather trousers. Her hair was an eye-catching shade of siren red and fell in artful ringlets around her petulant face, which brightened beneath the attention of the city's senior prosecutor.

Their tête-á-tête was interrupted by Juge Bernard's deep baritone.

"Thank you all for joining us at the reconstruction today," he said, in excellent English. "I believe my colleagues at the Brigade Criminelle have already briefed you, but the purpose of today is to ensure we understand fully what occurred in the small hours of Monday morning. A young woman's life is forever changed, and she will thank us for our efforts to uncover whoever took it upon themselves to cause her harm."

Like the procureur, Bernard had dressed for the occasion and was wearing another natty suit together with a crisp white shirt and tie that looked like a Hermès original. Both men struck Gregory as being ready for any conceivable situation, whether it be an impromptu briefing at Police Headquarters, or a press conference outside the Arc de Triomphe, and were more like politicians than law enforcers.

"Please wear protective shoe coverings before entering the crime scene—but I'd like to reassure you that the forensic team have finished their work and we've been cleared to enter. Once inside, we're going to step through what we know to have happened, according to the statements of those present here," Bernard said. "It may be that one of you remembers something new or wishes to amend what you have already told us. If that's the case, we urge you to speak up as soon as possible."

He nodded to Durand, who moved forward to open the door to Room 30. When people began to file inside, Gregory felt a slight pressure on his arm, holding him back.

"Who are you?" Madeleine whispered. "Why are you here?"

Gregory looked at her for a long moment, tracing the lines of her face and committing it to memory.

"I'm a criminal profiler," he replied softly. "I help the police to understand the kind of mind that commits crimes like these, so they can focus their investigation and narrow their pool of suspects. Back in England, I work with the most violent and disturbed criminals who've been detained by the courts."

Most nights, I can't sleep. Their stories haunt me, just like my mother, he almost said.

Madeleine snatched her hand away, and something twisted in his gut, which he steadfastly ignored. He told himself that he welcomed the rejection, because it would save him the trouble later on.

Here, in the cold light of day, she needed to understand the kind of man he was—and not just because they were part of the same police investigation and should keep a professional distance. Treating warped minds and trying to ease their torment was not a task for the faint-hearted— nor was the work of a profiler, who carried the details of hundreds of violent cases in the recesses of his mind. They took up every inch of emotional space, filling the gaping holes that might otherwise force him to seek answers to unanswered questions about his own psyche—or a person to share them with.

It was a solitary occupation and the sooner she understood that, the better.

"We'd better go inside," he said, and stepped back to allow her to precede him.

The interior of Room 30 still bore the shadows of Camille Duquette's attack.

The forensic team had removed many of its physical trappings, including the bedspread and the large Persian rug where she'd been found, and there was a lingering smell of chemicals as they stepped over the threshold. While Procureur Segal launched into a spiel about confidentiality and other legislative matters that were probably very important, Gregory focused on the details of the room.

It was a light, rectangular space, decorated in shades of cream, gold and pale duck egg blue. Small mirrored panels had been fitted to the walls with a nod to the Hall of Mirrors at the Palace of Versailles, which might have been tacky anywhere else in the world, but seemed entirely in keeping with the character of the hotel. His eye caught Madeleine's in one of those panels but she looked away, giving her full attention to the prosecutor. Gregory continued to study the room, which was dominated by a large canopied bed on the interior wall, facing two tall sash windows framed by heavy silk curtains. An open doorway led to a white marble bathroom, whilst another doorway had been cut into the wall beside it and decorated to match the panelling. Presumably, it led to Juliette's room next door, for there was a similar interconnecting doorway on the opposite wall leading off to Madeleine's room. There was the usual assortment of occasional furniture, and a set of slim double doors led onto a veranda, which held a bistro table and two chairs. It had an iron railing running along three sides to prevent accidental falls, but no ladders or exterior stairs that would make for an easy access point.

Gregory peeled away from the group and walked over to one of the windows. Outside, there was a grassy courtyard that served as an overflow seating area for the hotel's restaurant. It was accessible from the ground floor and through an elegant archway via the road, where passers-by could stop into the garden café tucked away from the hustle and bustle. Directly opposite Camille's room on the other side of the courtyard was the exterior wall of a large office building. During the day, with the sunlight bouncing off its windows, it was impossible to see beyond the glass. He imagined the same would be true if he were standing in the office building looking back across to the room where they now stood.

"*In a moment, we will ask you to return to your rooms and await the sound of a simulated crash…*"

Gregory dimly heard Segal's voice going over the running order of the reconstruction, and made a conscious effort to block it out. In his mind's eye, he pictured the crime scene photographs and imagined how Camille's room might have looked silhouetted against the night sky, its lights burning like a beacon.

"Were the curtains closed when the police team arrived?" he asked, of nobody in particular.

Conversation stalled at the untimely interruption.

"Pardon?" Segal snapped.

"I asked whether the curtains were open or closed when you found her," Gregory repeated.

Segal was not a man accustomed to interruptions.

"Closed," he said.

When nothing more was forthcoming, Segal directed the witnesses back to their respective rooms and told them to await a simulated crash, following which they should go through the motions of what they did on Monday night. It seemed a farcical experiment, in Gregory's view; little more than a box-ticking exercise so the Commissaire would be able to say that progress was being made—but at least it enabled him to see the layout of the crime scene and to meet some of the key players in the drama. With one obvious exception, they were all exactly as he'd imagined them to be.

Durand waited until the witnesses left, and then picked up the conversation.

"Why did you want to know about the curtains?" he asked. "Why do they matter?"

"A couple of reasons," Gregory replied. "The first is that, if the attacker planned a long, ritualistic kill, they'd have been far more likely to close the curtains to ensure absolute privacy and reduce the chances of being seen. The second is that, if the attacker wanted to plan their approach or spy on Camille ahead of the attack, it would be easier to do that if her room was lit up against a dark sky. It would be like watching a movie."

"The curtains were closed when we found her," Segal repeated, with a touch of excitement. "That confirms our original theory, that the intention was to kill Camille. Perhaps her attacker was interrupted."

"It's something to bear in mind," Gregory corrected. "I wouldn't say it was confirmation of anything."

But Segal was undeterred.

"Is there anything else you can tell us?"

Gregory had the unpleasant feeling he was being told to dance to an invisible fiddle, and his eyes flashed a warning.

"I told you at the start, I'm not clairvoyant. Profiling isn't a replacement for police work."

He swept a hand around the room.

"Somebody could have watched Camille through the window, but that's speculation, not evidence. Have you made enquiries at the office building over there?"

Three heads turned to look out of the window, and Durand made a hasty note.

"The statements gathered from the people in Camille's life are also incomplete," Gregory said. "There's no information about their impressions of her as a person; nothing but a bland recollection of dates and times. In our current predicament, we need all the information we can get, which will also help her psychiatrist to know how to speak to her and begin to draw her out."

Bernard exchanged a word with Durand, instructing him to begin a process of re-interviewing witnesses, and Gregory was surprised once again by the chain of command that removed the police inspector's ability to take charge of his own investigation.

"If no obvious traces of the assailant have been found, that would suggest a careful personality, somebody who took the time to plan and make provision; he or she would have to bring a bag, unless they were also staying at the hotel."

Durand was a quick study.

"We're in the process of completing background checks on all the people staying at the hotel," he said. "It will take time, for some of them."

"What are you saying?" Bernard demanded. "You think this is an inside job?"

He made a scoffing sound in the back of his throat.

"The attack was sadistic, *monsieur*. The act of a raging madman, not somebody who planned ahead."

Gregory gave a slight shake of his head.

"The two aren't mutually exclusive," he said, and began to pace around the room, getting a feel for the space before coming to stand beside one of the mirrored panels, which had been broken—presumably when Camille's head had been thrust against the glass. "Ever heard of the BTK killer?"

He referred to the infamous American serial killer whose moniker stood for 'Bind, Torture, Kill'.

"He planned meticulously, stalking his victims, learning their routines before choosing the moment to strike. It's a method he perfected over a number of years, during which time he could go for long periods without activity. He isn't the only example of how control can be exercised along with a complete lack of it."

"You think somebody could be targeting models like Camille?" Bernard asked him. "If that's the case, we have a much bigger problem than we thought."

Segal let out a muttered expletive, no doubt thinking of the bureaucratic circus that would ensue, if that prediction turned out to be correct.

"Anything is possible," Gregory said. "But it would be unsafe to speculate without knowing more about the victim, as I've already told you. To determine whether the attack was opportunistic, or targeted, we need to know more about Camille. The majority of attackers are known to their victims, and cases of stranger-attacks are relatively rare by comparison. Let's rule out the first option, before we jump to the second."

He turned to Mathis Durand, who was scratching the top of his head with the chewed end of a biro.

"When we're done here, I think it's time I paid Camille a visit."

"She still hasn't spoken," Durand warned him.

"Then there's nothing to lose."

CHAPTER 7

The wound was long and jagged.

It ran like a fault line across Camille Duquette's face; an angry, purpling welt that ruptured her flawless skin almost from lip to hairline. Gregory's eyes followed the line of it from his position beside her bed, where he and Durand were seated on a couple of chairs they'd dragged in from the small kitchen-diner next door.

"*Elle a été comme ça pendant la majeure partie de la journée,*" the nurse told them.

"She says Camille's been like this for most of the day," Durand translated, needlessly.

The nurse was one of two capable-looking women of around sixty who had been hired by Maison Leroux at great expense to provide round-the-clock care.

Gregory leaned forward, resting his forearms lightly on his knees.

"Camille?" he said softly, and reverted to French. "*Camille, tu m'entends?*"

He could feel Durand's eyes boring into the side of his skull and, assuming correctly that his cover was now blown, surrendered himself to speaking fluently.

"*Can you hear me, Camille? My name is Alexander Gregory. I'm a psychologist, from England.*"

Her eyes remained closed, but her lashes flickered.

"Camille, I know you can hear me," he said, continuing to speak in the same, even tone. "The doctors say there's nothing wrong with your hearing, so I'd like you to listen to me, for a moment. I know you've been through a terrible experience, and that you're frightened and in pain. But there are people who want to help you. Doctor Gonzalez and the police, your nurse, me…we all want to help you to find your family and the person who did this to you."

Her head jerked against the pillow, but her eyes remained shut.

"What pain medication is she taking?" Gregory asked, wondering why she had been so heavily sedated. It was usual for opioids to be reduced after forty-eight hours, to minimise the potential for dependency, but the woman still seemed catatonic.

"Doctor Gonzalez had to sedate her this morning, and gave instructions for her to remain so until he returns to check on her this afternoon," the nurse told him, and rattled off details of the strong cocktail of drugs Camille had been prescribed.

"What happened this morning?" Gregory prodded.

"She tried to run off," the nurse replied, in a flat, no-nonsense tone. "She was very distressed."

Durand reared forward.

"*What*? Why wasn't I informed of this?"

"Doctor Gonzalez spoke to one of your superiors," she said, and leaned forward to dab Camille's mouth with a moist flannel. "Perhaps he forgot to tell you."

Durand pushed back from his chair and excused himself, already pulling out his mobile phone and muttering a stream of colourful obscenities.

In the silence that followed, Gregory watched the nurse start to clean Camille's wound with small pieces of gauze.

"It needs a fresh bandage," she tutted.

Gregory let the woman finish her careful task, and listened with half an ear to the voluble conversation Durand was conducting with either Bernard or Segal in the hallway outside.

"How did she try to leave?" he asked.

The nurse rolled back her sleeve to reveal a long scratch on her forearm.

"This happened when I tried to restrain her," she said, with a disapproving look for the young woman who lay motionless against the white covers. "I came in at seven this morning to relieve the night nurse, who told me she'd been sleeping like a lamb all night."

She puffed out her ample chest.

"Lamb? She's more like a fox, this one," she said, giving her patient the beady eye. "One moment, she is calm and

quiet. I go into the kitchen for water and come back to find…
poof! She's out of the bed, dragging herself towards the door,
shouting like a madwoman—"

"Just a moment," Gregory said. "She was *shouting*?"

The nurse looked at him as though he were a simpleton.

"Isn't that what I said? I tell you, the girl was shouting and
screaming like a banshee, trying to claw her way out. She
could have hurt herself."

Durand re-joined them, wearing the look of a camel
who'd borne his final straw.

"Did I hear something about shouting?" he asked.

But Gregory was determined to ask the most important
question of all, while it was relatively fresh in the woman's
mind.

"Please, tell me, what did she say?" he asked urgently.
"When she screamed, what words did she say?"

The nurse shook her head.

"There were no words, *monsieur*," she replied. "There was
only sound, like a baby's cry."

Gregory and Durand stayed a few minutes longer, while
Camille remained in a fretful sleep.

"She is still beautiful, *non*?"

Gregory turned to look at the inspector, then back at the
woman on the bed.

"Yes," he agreed quietly. "In the fickle world she aspired to be a part of before her attack, I doubt she'll be seen as a great beauty any longer. But now, she's something much more."

Durand thought about it.

"A survivor," he said.

"*Exactement*," Gregory murmured, with a smile.

Durand leaned back in his chair and folded fleshy arms across his chest.

"You were sneaky there, my friend," he said, referring to Gregory's fluency in French. "I ask myself whether there's anything else you're not telling me."

Gregory sighed.

"You know about Madeleine," he realised, and supposed his surprise at seeing her at the reconstruction earlier that day had been the giveaway. "I was planning to tell you."

"So? Tell me," Durand invited. "Don't spare any detail, either."

Gregory gave him a withering look.

"I met Madeleine Paquet for the first time last night, at the Coco Caverne jazz club, where she sings using the stage name 'Margot'. I had no idea Margot and Madeleine were the same person until she opened the door to her room at the Hôtel Violette."

Durand cleared his throat and prepared to ask an indelicate question with as much delicacy as he could muster.

Which wasn't much.

"How *well* did you get to know her?"

It gave Alex a perverse kind of satisfaction to disappoint him.

"Not as well as you might imagine," he said, testily. "Margot—or Madeleine—finished her set at around two, and we stayed at the club listening to the other musicians and talking until shortly after four, when the place closed. At no time did she mention her other profession, and nor did I mention my work as a criminal profiler."

Just two people, he thought. *Enjoying one another's company.*

"I made sure she found a taxi and was safely inside, before walking back to my hotel in the Rue Lepic."

"And…that's all?"

"Scout's honour," Gregory drawled. Though he'd been sorely tempted, he had to admit.

"*Quoi?*"

"Never mind," he muttered. "I agreed to meet her tomorrow night, at her next gig. It happens to be at the Café Laurent, which is attached to the hotel where I'm staying."

Durand waggled a finger and let out another of his bawdy laughs that reminded Gregory of an old actor from the Carry On movies. He would have said as much, but he suspected the intrepid inspector would fail to understand the reference.

"I see, I see," he said, still chuckling to himself. "Do you plan to keep the date?"

"Of course not," Gregory said. "It would be inappropriate, given what I now know about her relationship to the investigation."

Durand scratched the side of his nose, then shrugged.

"The investigation won't last forever," he said. "And, whether you admit it or not, you're as human as the rest of us, *mon ami*."

Gregory couldn't argue with that.

"Are you happy for me to continue to work on the investigation?" he asked.

Durand didn't answer directly.

"I've already made a recommendation to Procureur Segal that Doctor Gonzalez be removed from his present duties," he said. "Not only did he fail to contact me directly to report Camille's attempt to abscond, he also failed to report that she had made her first sounds, albeit no words were spoken. In a case of this sensitivity, where each piece of information must be treated as valuable, it was a serious failing on his part."

He nodded towards the woman on the bed.

"Besides, Gonzalez has had three days to try to assess her speech and reverse the trauma, with no progress whatsoever."

Gregory was a strong proponent of slow and steady progress with patients in general, but it was equally true that speedy action was sometimes required.

"Would you like me to help you find another specialist?" he asked, already wondering who he might know and could recommend to the police.

Durand merely smiled.

"I've already found one."

The penny dropped, very quickly, and Gregory held up his hands.

"Now, wait, just a minute. I agreed to help as a profiler, not as a psychologist. She needs intensive therapy, which I can't possibly provide—"

"You said yourself, the victim is the most important clue of all," Durand argued.

Gregory had to give him points for that.

"I did, and I still believe that. But, if I take Camille Duquette on as a patient, I'd need to seek permission from my employer back in the UK. Even if they agree, I would owe Camille a duty of care that might conflict with my work as a profiler."

Durand considered the point, and then gave another one of his maddening shrugs.

"The most important thing is to get her to talk," he said. "If you can help us to do that, you can leave the rest in our hands."

Gregory looked over at the sleeping beauty and found himself wondering what lay behind her eyes, which he knew from her photographs to be a deep, aquamarine blue. If he took her on as a private patient, he could authorise a reduced level of medication that would relieve any physical discomfort without leaving her comatose. Perhaps then she might open her eyes and consider talking to him.

He came to a decision.

"I'll agree to work with her for the rest of this week, with the proviso that you find a more appropriate long-term clinician to take over her care."

Durand held out his hand.

"Agreed.

CHAPTER 8

When it became clear that no further progress would be made with Camille that day, Gregory gave instructions for her medication to be reduced to a more appropriate level, leaving Durand to break the bad news to Doctor Gonzalez. Once that unenviable task was complete, they left Camille in the capable hands of her nurse and went off in search of other clues to her identity.

The sun had dipped low in the sky by the time they emerged from the apartment building, and the two men decided to walk the short journey to the Champ de Mars, which was the large park running from the foot of the Eiffel Tower all the way to the École Militaire, on the south side of the Seine. It also happened to be the chosen venue for that evening's catwalk show, and an enormous marquee had been erected similar to the one at the Jardin des Tuileries, on the other side of the river.

As they rounded a corner, Gregory stopped and stared.

It shouldn't have been beautiful, he thought, but it was.

With shards of hazy afternoon sunlight filtering through its latticed iron beams, Gustave Eiffel's tower was an impressive sight to behold.

"Do you ever get tired of looking at it?" Gregory asked of his surly new friend.

Mathis Durand tipped his head up to look, then made a sound a bit like a raspberry.

"*Pas mal*," he declared. "Me, I would like to see the Burj Khalifa, in Dubai. They say it's the tallest building in the world."

Gregory smiled and thought there was a saying about familiarity breeding contempt, and perhaps that was true. He couldn't remember the last time he'd admired the Tower of London or Big Ben.

"Tell me about the people we're going to see," he said, as they entered the park and spotted a large white tent taking up an area of grass in the central walkway.

Durand rubbed his hands together to warm them, then stuck them in his armpits.

"During Fashion Week, there are a number of different venues each night," he said. "They don't belong to one fashion house in particular, though they pay to reserve the best spaces, such as here in the Champ de Mar."

Gregory read between the lines.

"To reserve one of the better spots, you'd need to have plenty of money," he said. "I take it Maison Leroux isn't doing too badly?"

Durand nodded.

"It's a newer label, but fast-growing and with plenty of private backing," he explained. "Armand Leroux was a financier before he retired, and Gabrielle's father is in the oil business. For them, it's always the best of everything."

Gregory nodded and thought of his own father, who had been a banker and now lived a very comfortable life in a large house overlooking Lake Geneva, or so he'd heard.

He hadn't set eyes on the man in more than twenty years.

"Scandals like these can work both ways," Durand continued. "It can help to drum up a bit of extra publicity, but it can also scare people away. To Leroux, Camille may be both an asset and a liability."

"Which is why they've squirrelled her away," Gregory muttered.

They passed a small news stand, featuring several papers and magazines displaying Camille's picture, taken from the publicity photo in her police file. The story of her attack and subsequent silence no longer occupied a full-page spread, and had instead been relegated to a smaller column, but at least her ordeal was still newsworthy.

The privilege of beauty, in action.

"I take it nobody has come forward yet following the police appeal?" he asked. "Nobody claiming to know Camille?"

Durand shook his head.

"We've had the usual crazies," he said, and Gregory's lips twitched. "Strange women claiming to be her mother, old men claiming to be her husband or father, but none of them check out. It's always the same with cases like these—it's a question of sorting through all the bullshit."

They paused while Gregory bought a couple of short coffees, enjoying the scent of roasted beans as the liquid percolated through a machine that had been built into the back of a tiny, three-wheeled van.

"The Leroux are what you might call a power couple," Durand said, once they were armed with brown cardboard cups. "They're in every social column, they attend all the best parties and events. Their clothes are worn at the Oscars and the Golden Globes, the Césars and at Cannes. Officially, they're a wealthy, happily married couple."

"But?"

Durand inclined his head.

"*But* the gossip columns say that Armand has an eye for the ladies."

Gregory thought privately that the statistical propensity for infidelity amongst French men was hardly newsworthy.

"If that's true, it must be difficult working with a smorgasbord of beautiful women every day," he said. "But infidelity isn't a crime."

Durand shook his head.

"*Rendre grâce á Dieu*," he muttered, as they drew nearer to the site where the marquee had been pitched.

Security railings had been set up around the perimeter of the marquee, manned by dark-suited, ex-military security staff. A long, red carpet had been laid out and ran from a roadside entrance up to a canopied portico. Torches had been staked into the ground and, once lit, would create a mock runway for all those who entered.

"I bet I can guess what you're thinking," Durand said, with a touch of smugness. "You're wondering whether the lovely Madeleine will be waiting for you in there, *non*?"

Gregory shook his head.

"Actually, I was wondering what they'll do if it starts to rain."

<hr />

The skies remained cold but cloudless and, as the sun eventually slipped into the horizon and the torches were lit, Gregory and Durand entered the backstage area of the marquee. There, they were faced with a cacophony of chattering men and women—well over a hundred, taking into account all the hairdressers, make-up artists and photographers, design staff and technicians who made up the fabric of Maison Leroux.

Durand seemed momentarily dumbfounded by the concentration of so much glamour in so small a space, and Gregory took it upon himself to do the talking.

"Excuse me, we're looking for Mme Leroux?"

The hairdresser he'd spoken to waved a roller brush in the direction of an anteroom that was partially hidden behind a set of artificial conifers.

"*Là dedans*," she said.

Gregory thanked her and then nudged Durand forward.

They made their way through an open plan dressing space with banks of chairs and mirrors, each bearing the name of the model who would be stationed there, alongside a number of photographs depicting the various 'looks' they would be modelling that evening. On the other side of the room, there were rows of clothing rails with similar name tags attached.

As they passed by, Gregory caught sight of a slender woman disappearing into the forest of silks and satins, and could have sworn it was Madeleine.

Has my boy got a crush?

At the sound of his mother's voice, Gregory's heart began to pound against the wall of his chest, while his skin broke into a clammy sweat.

He heard her laughter so clearly, she might have been standing beside him.

Unable to stop himself, Gregory swung around to check over his shoulder, eyes wide and searching.

But, of course, there was nobody there except a roomful of fashionable people, none of whom was his mother.

"Alex?"

Turning back, he found Durand looking at him strangely.

"Is everything all right?"

Alex consciously relaxed his shoulders.

"Fine," he said. "Just a bit hot in here, that's all."

Durand's small, mole-like eyes continued to search his face and Gregory had the uncomfortable sensation that he was trying to peel back the layers of his mind, to see what lay buried in its deepest core.

Was this what his patients felt like, as they sat opposite him in the consulting room?

He was saved from answering any probing questions by the sound of a man's high-pitched voice carrying across the room.

"Where is he? Is *that* him?"

A man of around Durand's age sauntered towards them and, even without the professional camera swinging at his hip, Gregory would have guessed the newcomer to be a photographer. There could be no mistaking the uniform of form-fitting black jeans and shirt—with a couple of buttons left open at the collar—not to mention the loosely-draped scarf and an assortment of beaded jewellery that looked so cheap that Gregory could be reasonably sure it was eye-wateringly expensive.

Alex scarcely had time to prepare himself before the man grabbed his chin in a vice-like grip and turned his face this way and that, then stepped back to run a critical eye over the rest of his physique.

"You don't look anything like your portfolio," he said accusingly. "You're an inch shorter, for one thing, you need a haircut, and you should have had more sleep. But…perhaps we can do something with the rest of you."

"Thank you," Gregory said, gravely, while Durand goggled at them both. "However, I think there's been a mistake. I'm not part of the show, I'm here with the police."

He gestured towards Durand, who took out his identification card. The photographer looked at him as if he were an unusual sort of specimen, then peered at the writing on the card.

"Mathis Durand, Brigade Criminelle," he read. "I spoke to your colleagues the other day. They came to take statements from all of us."

While his head was turned, Gregory noticed for the first time that the entire right side of the photographer's neck was covered in an old burns scar, which had been concealed beneath the folds of his voluminous scarf. He wondered how it had happened—nosiness being an active by-product of his profession.

"And you are Leon Boucher, I presume?"

The photographer inclined his head in answer to Durand's question, with the complacent air of one who expected his name to be recognised instantly.

"I am Leon," he said, and then turned his attention back to Gregory. "A pity. I would have liked to do something with your face, perhaps in monotone, playing with the shadows."

Alex was momentarily lost for words.

"Doctor Gregory will be far too busy helping us with our investigation," Durand said, taking pity on him.

"Ah, yes. Poor Camille," Leon sighed. "Such a waste."

"Did you know her well?" Gregory asked, since the man seemed to be in a talkative mood.

"Hardly at all," he replied. "It's like I said to the other inspector, Gabrielle sent her to me for a test shoot, to see if she had the right look on film. It's one thing to see a pretty woman on the street, but it doesn't mean they'll take a good photo," he added. "Anyway, she came into my studio a couple of weeks ago with frizzy hair and heavy make-up, looking like some little *putain*—which is what I told her before I sent her into the bathroom to scrub it all off."

Gregory began to realise what Durand had meant about the fashion world being cutthroat.

"What were your impressions of her, aside from that?" Durand asked him.

Leon lifted a bony shoulder.

"She was…confident," he said, meaningfully. "She had no modelling experience but, after a little direction, it was as though she'd been in front of the camera her whole life. Gabrielle was very pleased with the images and decided to hire Camille for several editorials we had coming up, as well as Fashion Week."

"Did you like her?" Gregory asked, simply.

Leon looked away.

"It isn't my job to like the models I photograph," he said, evasively.

"Honesty is best," Durand murmured. "We're investigating attempted murder, not a parking fine, my friend."

Leon swept his fringe out of his eyes and, as he did, Gregory caught sight of some scratches on his inner wrist.

"Hurt yourself?" he asked.

The photographer looked down and then gave a self-deprecating laugh, tugging the cuff of his shirt to cover them.

"That? It was my cat, Marie Antoinette. She is a beast, who rules my apartment with an iron claw—just like her namesake."

Gregory smiled, but it didn't quite reach his eyes.

"You were telling us whether you liked Camille."

The smile faded from Leon's eyes.

"What do you want me to say? That she was demanding and difficult? She was," he said. "I told her she should wise up and remember there were many other girls who could step into her shoes, just like *that*."

He clicked his fingers, which were covered in silver rings.

"The truth is, she had something rare that was unpractised but very natural," he said, grudgingly. "She had a face…it was the perfect canvas. With one look, she could be the innocent ingenue. With another, she could be a vixen."

That was the second time somebody had used that particular metaphor as a descriptor for Camille, Gregory thought, and he was finding it hard to reconcile with the quiet, shrunken woman he'd seen huddled on the bed less than an hour before.

"She was an extrovert," Leon continued. "Very… *experimental*."

He seemed to roll the word around on his tongue, and his lips spread into a lazy, affected smile that Gregory disliked intensely.

"The photographs made the bosses happy, which is all that matters. But, if you're asking me whether she was somebody I'd go out of my way to help, then the answer is 'no'. She was an entitled little madam, even by this industry's standards."

Leon gave an irritable shrug.

"Ambition is not a bad thing, but Camille carried an air about her, as if she deserved to be here amongst people who have worked hard to claw their way inside. I wonder whether she'll look back on it one day and regret how she behaved, once the scars heal."

He drew himself in, seemingly aware that he had said too much. But, before he could leave, Durand asked a final question.

"Did Camille tell you anything about herself? Her family, or where she had come from? Her previous job, for example?"

But the photographer shook his head.

"It's like I said on Monday. I wouldn't remember, even if she had. I see three, four models a day at least, and some of them chatter to help with their nerves. I tell them to be quiet, or I let them talk to themselves. Either way, my mind is on my work. Why don't you ask Gabrielle? She's the one who discovered her."

Leon raised a hand to wave at someone across the room.

"And now, you must excuse me, gentlemen. As you can see, I'm very busy."

They watched him saunter away again, air-kissing people as he went, then Durand turned to Gregory and stared closely at his face.

"What?" Alex prompted him.

"It's nothing, I was only trying to imagine what you would look like in monochrome. Perhaps with a little shadow, here and there?"

Gregory muttered something uncomplimentary in gutter French, which brought a delighted laugh from the inspector.

"See? Already, you're becoming one of us. Come, let me introduce you to your new employer."

While Gregory and Durand tried to find their bearings in the world of high fashion, Eva Bisset stared out of a window at the people passing by in cars or on bikes, and wondered what Jean-Pierre had done with her scooter. Ever since she'd told him about the baby, he'd insisted that she was to make no more delivery rounds—and had been furious when she'd flouted that edict.

The scooter had been confiscated after that.

If she closed her eyes, she could feel the wind against her face as she motored through the streets—but she could also smell an earthy mix of turmeric and ground paprika as the meat sizzled in the kitchen and seeped through the walls to where she now stood, with her nose pressed against the glass.

She raised a shaking hand to scrub away the tears that leaked from her eyes and ran down her neck, blurring her vision.

The baby was gone.

She'd known, the moment it happened; she'd felt its tiny life being stolen away from her, along with the dreams she had of being its mother, leaving nothing but an empty, raw space in her womb.

Jean-Pierre would be furious when he found out.

It wasn't my fault, she longed to tell him.

But she didn't know where he'd gone, and was afraid of what he might do when he returned.

She watched a pair of giggling women pass by, their skinny bodies sheathed in expensive wool coats, and thought of the fashion people who were swarming the city with their plastic hearts and plastic smiles.

She hated them.

She felt a small twinge of pain low in her abdomen and was reminded again of just how much.

CHAPTER 9

When they entered the inner sanctum belonging to Gabrielle and Armand Leroux, it was like crossing the Arctic Circle. From ceiling to floor, everything was white—including the leather sofa upon which Armand reclined, with his belly spilling over tight white trousers and a pristine white shirt that strained at the buttons as he snored. They didn't notice Gabrielle at first, her platinum blonde hair and pale skin camouflaged by her surroundings until she stepped away from the static backdrop and moved towards them.

"*Inspecteur, c'est bon de vous revoir, mais j'ai bien peur que vous nous ayez supris au mauvais moment...*"

"*Pardon, Madame,* can we speak in English, for the benefit of our guest?" Durand interrupted her, and smiled blandly at Alex. "This is Doctor Gregory, who is lending his services as a criminal profiler to the investigation, as well as his expertise in the field of psychology to work with Camille over the coming days."

She turned and gave him an automatic once-over, which seemed to be the habit of those working in her industry.

"So good to meet you," she murmured, almost inaudibly. "It's dreadful what's happened to poor Camille, and we're all devastated to lose her at such a crucial time. Aren't we, Armand?"

The man must have had hearing like a bat, Gregory thought, because he awakened instantly from what appeared to have been a very deep sleep and proceeded to swing his considerable bulk off the edge of the sofa.

"What did you say, my love?"

Armand was a man comfortably in his sixties, with a mop of carefully quaffed grey hair and the bloodshot eyes of one who had enjoyed a heavy drinking session the night before. He was at least forty years older than his wife, who didn't seem to mind as he stumbled across the room towards them and draped a heavy arm over her slight shoulders.

"Ah, Inspector Durand! You should have woken me up sooner," he chided Gabrielle, and pinched her button nose in a gesture that left the other two men in the room feeling vaguely nauseated.

"I didn't want to wake you, my darling," his wife crooned.

Durand cleared his throat.

"I was just introducing your wife to Doctor Gregory, who's an expert in criminal profiling and has agreed to assist us while we investigate the attempted murder of Camille Duquette."

Armand's eyes widened theatrically, and he surged forward to grasp Gregory's hand in both of his own sweaty palms.

"Monsieur, you are most welcome," he gushed. "I can't tell you what a worry it's been to us, these past few days. When I think of how frightened Camille must have been…I have a daughter myself, from a previous marriage. In the absence of her own family, Gabrielle and I knew it was only right that we should look after her. Isn't that so, *ma cherie*?"

Armand dropped Gregory's hand and drew his wife in for a smacking kiss, while Alex surreptitiously wiped his palm on the back of his trousers. If this was a man renowned for his infidelities, he certainly put on a good show. But then, Armand wouldn't be the first to have cultivated the art of good showmanship.

"Have you made any progress with the case?" Gabrielle asked. "How is Camille doing?"

"We're following all leads," Durand said, repeating a line that must surely be universal to detectives the world over. "Camille is in a stable condition, but she still hasn't spoken."

Gabrielle closed her eyes, put a delicate hand on her heart—which was encased in a long, floating column of bridal white—and whispered a prayer.

"We were hoping to ask you both some follow-up questions," Durand said, drawing out his little reporter's notebook and another half-eaten biro from the inner pocket of his coat.

"We can only spare you a few minutes, I'm afraid," Armand warned him. "The show is due to start in a couple of hours, and we must go and check all the preparations are in order and begin to greet our guests."

"I must also check the models," Gabrielle murmured, and then raised a hand.

A mousy-haired assistant seemed to materialise from nowhere, bearing an enormous leather folder in one hand and a mobile phone in the other.

"*Oui, Madame*?"

Gabrielle proceeded to issue a series of brusque instructions to her assistant, and Gregory was interested to note the marked change to the tone of her voice as she did so.

Still waters ran deep, with that one.

The assistant left with a deferential bow, and when Gabrielle turned back to the others in the room, she was all breathless smiles again.

"Please, come and have a seat."

She led them across to the sofa where Armand had recently caught forty winks and perched herself on the edge.

"How can we help you?"

Durand dived straight in.

"You say in your statement that you know nothing about Camille Duquette, other than the information she provided to your payroll department. Is that correct?"

"Well, it was all quite last minute, you see. Camille only joined us a couple of weeks ago," Armand said, defensively.

"You didn't think to enquire about her employment history?" Gregory asked.

"Monsieur, perhaps you don't appreciate the nature of our business," Gabrielle told him, and her voice was once again all honey. "No particular qualification or experience is required to become a model, even at *this* level."

She raised both hands to gesture at the opulence around them.

"Camille was blessed with a rare kind of beauty," she continued, speaking firmly in the past tense. "That alone is not unusual. I've met countless young men and women whose faces are perfectly symmetrical, their skin flawless, their bodies smooth and slim. But there's no…"

"*Je ne sais quoi*?" Gregory drawled.

"Exactly," she said. "Camille is an intelligent young woman, and it shows in her pictures. She was like a chameleon, able to adapt herself. That isn't something that can be taught, Doctor Gregory. I recognised it, the first time I saw her, and asked if she was interested in a new career. I sent her to Leon, who told me she was a natural."

She crossed her legs at the ankle, very demurely.

"Deportment, the art of how to walk…that can all be taught," she said. "We gave her a crash course, and by the end of the day she was walking like a duchess. I mean it when I tell you, she's a great loss to Maison Leroux."

It was a pretty little speech, Gregory thought, but she gave away very little.

Apparently, Durand thought the same thing.

"You say you discovered Camille on the street—can you tell me exactly where and what she was doing at the time?"

Gabrielle let out a tinkling laugh.

"I'm sorry, Inspector, but you must understand I'm a very busy woman. I can't remember exactly where I was when I first saw Camille. Outside our building on the Rue Saint-

Honoré? After dining at Le Pré Catelan? Really, who can say? As for her previous work, why on Earth should I care?"

The logic of it was breathtakingly simple, Gregory acknowledged.

"You cannot possibly be expected to remember something so trifling, my love," Armand said, pressing another kiss to her palm. "Can she, Inspector?"

"Actually, it would be extremely helpful if you would try, Madame," Durand said tightly.

Gabrielle's eyes turned flat.

"Well, I've told you, I can't remember," she said. "Perhaps, *messieurs*, you should not be wasting any further time here, when a would-be killer remains at large."

Gregory raised an eyebrow, fascinated by her transformation from the insipid woman they'd first met.

"Very well," he said. "Perhaps you could give us some general observations about Camille's character prior to the attack. What was she like? Did the other models like her?"

Armand lifted his shoulders.

"In a business such as ours, one has to expect a certain degree of competition," he said, and Gabrielle gave a haughty nod of assent. "Men and women scrap to win the best jobs, and most have been on the circuit a little while, whereas Camille had not. Perhaps some felt she hadn't earned her place at the table, as it were."

"Anyone specifically?" Gregory shot back.

They looked uncomfortable, but then Gabrielle whispered something in her husband's ear.

"I'm sure she didn't mean that, my love," he murmured, and then turned back to them. "My wife has just reminded me of an occasion when one of our other models, Juliette, got into...let's say a little fight with Camille. She accused her of having taken some jewellery belonging to her, which, of course, Camille strongly denied."

"Who did you believe?" Gregory asked.

"Well, since nothing was found on Camille's person, or in her bag, we assumed Juliette was stirring up trouble and had simply lost the necklace," Armand said. "We don't concern ourselves with day to day squabbles, but Leon told us this was the second time such an accusation had been made."

"Oh? When was the first?" Durand asked.

"I understand another of the models accused Camille of having taken some perfume and a small brooch, which was of sentimental value," Armand said. "But none of this has been proven at all, Inspector, and no report was ever made to the police. It could very well be an example of the kind of bullying that, sadly, can happen in a small world such as ours."

There was a moment's pause.

"Do you think anybody at Maison Leroux disliked Camille enough to wish her harm?" Gregory asked.

"Absolutely not," Gabrielle said, firmly. "I am convinced it was a stranger, perhaps some poor unfortunate who was fixated on Camille. Jealousy is an ugly trait, Doctor, but the people in my company are like *family*. Besides, do you imagine any of the models on our books have any need to feel jealous of one another?"

Gregory looked at her for a long moment, thinking that the world of high fashion was a veritable breeding ground for insecurity and, if it was true that her husband was known to have a predilection for beautiful younger women—such as herself—then Gabrielle Leroux would be just as susceptible as anyone. After all, what better way to extinguish her husband's ardour than to destroy the thing that had ignited it?

"Jealousy is, indeed, an ugly trait," he said quietly. "Sadly, in my experience, it's one that crosses the boundaries of society and transcends physical beauty, Madame Leroux. It comes from a much darker place—inside the human heart."

When Gregory and Durand stepped into the night air a short time later, the cold hit them like an icy wall, and came as a welcome relief from the overheated interior of the marquee. They were ushered out of the perimeter gate and, as it clicked shut behind them, each man was left with the strong impression of having returned from a surreal, fantastical place where nothing was quite as it seemed.

They turned back to see torches blazing along the red-carpeted entranceway, which was lined on either side with rows of journalists and photographers who awaited the arrival of the first celebrity guests. Overhead, thousands of individual spotlights cloaked the Eiffel Tower in a cascade of shimmering white light, probably organised by Maison Leroux to coincide with their show.

"We could stay and watch," Durand offered, half-heartedly.

But Gregory shook his head.

"I've had my fill of fashion for one day," he said, and then hesitated. "Do you—ah, I was thinking of having some dinner?"

Durand gave him a manly slap on the back.

"Of course, *mon ami*. I know a good place."

CHAPTER 10

The 'good place' turned out to be Durand's little garden apartment.

It was part of a modern block of flats bordering La Chapelle and Saint-Denis, a residential area to the north of Paris which possessed the kind of purpose-built feel that reminded Gregory of garden cities like Welwyn Garden City or Milton Keynes in the UK—except with fewer roundabouts. There was little in the way of memorable architecture but, as they passed along the main road, he saw an enormous secondary school, new road surfaces and a hospital.

"It's getting better around here," Durand said, as they passed by a children's playground. "Not as bad as the old days."

"Seems to be a nice family area," Gregory agreed, then looked across at the police inspector. "Do you have any yourself? Family, I mean?"

It was by no means a given; of all the murder detectives he'd met in his time, only a few had been able to maintain a long-term committed relationship and it wasn't hard to understand why. The job was thankless and unforgiving, the kind only a small percentage of the population would be able to perform and still stay sane. Even then, most self-medicated with alcohol and that, together with long periods away from home, led to a toxic cycle that didn't usually lend itself to happy marriages.

And, to be brutally honest, he supposed the same could be said of his own situation.

But Durand surprised him.

"I have two children," he said. "A boy and a girl—both grown up now—and a wife, Sandrine, who looks after me, for her sins."

He led Gregory up to a modest front door.

"Sandrine! I've brought a visitor with me!"

Inside, the flat was warm and inviting, and smelled of roasting meat.

"Through here!"

They found Sandrine in the living room with a glass of wine and a book, which she put aside as they came in. She was a petite woman of around fifty, who sported an elegant silver-blonde bob and a pair of laughing brown eyes.

"You're earlier than I thought," she said, rising from her chair to bestow a kiss before turning to their guest.

"This is Doctor Alexander Gregory, a psychologist from England."

She gave him a peck on either cheek.

"You bring a psychologist home for dinner, Mathis? Are you trying to tell me something?"

Both men laughed.

"It's far too late for either of us, my love," Durand chuckled. "Alex is helping me with a case I'm working on at the moment, and he's in need of a good meal."

"Well, he's come to the right place."

Later, while Durand helped his wife clear away the dinner things, Gregory took a turn around the living room. A person's private domain was often revealing and, even at Southmoor, where patients were limited as to the personal possessions they could keep in their rooms, it was amazing how one space varied to the next. In the case of Mathis and Sandrine Durand, their living room reflected a life shared; an enormous, overstuffed bookcase occupied one wall, while another was covered in framed prints of their children, taken on birthdays and Christmases over the years.

There wasn't a police file or a criminology textbook in sight, which told him that Durand preferred to keep his work and home lives separate.

Wise man.

"That's my boy, Paul," Durand said, coming to stand beside him as they looked at the open, smiling face of a young man of nineteen or twenty. "He's training at the Academy to become a police officer, like his old man."

"You'll be able to show him the ropes," Gregory said.

Durand made a non-committal sound.

"There are better things to do with his life," he muttered.

"You wouldn't want him to join the Police Judiciaire or the Gendarmerie?"

Durand reached for a half-drunk bottle of wine and topped up their glasses.

"Paul thinks he'll be a hero," he said, and took a swig of wine. "I know better."

"You're old and crusty," his wife pointed out, coming to sit beside them. "Paul knows his own mind."

"Like his mother," Durand said, with a smile.

Talk turned to everything from politics to cuisine and back again, before Gregory realised that he'd spent a pleasant evening in the company of others without once feeling an urge to check the time.

Nevertheless, the hour was drawing late.

"Thank you for a wonderful dinner, Madame Durand," he said.

"Sandrine," she corrected him. "Come and visit us again, Alex."

Despite Gregory's protests, Durand insisted upon driving him back to his hotel—having stayed just below the legally acceptable amount of alcohol to operate a vehicle in those parts—and there ensued a kamikaze journey back into the centre of town.

"You have a lovely home," Gregory said, once his stomach had levelled itself out again.

"Thanks to Sandrine," Durand admitted. "Without her to come home to, without my kids, the job would be a lot harder. It was difficult when Paul and Eloise moved out."

"You miss them?"

"Of course," he said. "But they must find their own way in the world."

He didn't bat an eyelid as a cyclist veered into the road ahead, nor did he slow down, but simply jerked the wheel to avoid a collision.

"What about you, Alex? Is there anyone special to go home to?"

Gregory thought about making some flippant remark, but found himself telling the absolute truth.

"No," he said. "My work is all-consuming."

Durand gave him a strange look.

"The work we do…it's important, yes, but it should not *consume* us, *mon ami.*"

But it's the only thing that has any meaning in my life. The only thing I can trust will always be there, to fall back on. Not people. Not mothers, not fathers, wives or anything else in between. Not anything so fallible, and unreliable, as another human being.

Purpose.

A reason for being.

Those were the things he could count on, and by helping those in need, by finding compassion for them, he could begin to forgive all the others who had let him down.

But he said none of that.

"You're probably right," he murmured, and turned away to watch the passing lights of the city.

CHAPTER 11

Friday 27th September

The room was blindingly white and smelled of lemons.

Alex threw up a hand to shield his eyes, unable to see any shapes or hear any sounds.

Where was he?

The ground crunched beneath his feet, and he stumbled forward without any sense of direction, arms outstretched to cushion the blow if he should fall.

"Hello? Is anybody there?"

The words disappeared as soon as they left his lips, swallowed by the white space, which seemed to shift and change all around him, contracting in time to his own beating heart.

Alex turned around, and around again, but could see nothing except the same blinding white light.

I'm over here.

He stumbled over his own feet, seeking out his mother's voice.

You know me, don't you?

Yes, he knew her voice. It was the first sound he'd ever heard, but it would not be the last.

You know what you did, don't you?

"I tried to understand you…so I could forgive you," he whispered.

But there could be no forgiveness; the crime was too great, and the grief too painful.

What if you were wrong?

Her voice crawled into his mind, coaxing and insidious.

Look in the mirror. What do you see?

Suddenly, he found himself inside a long, gilded hallway, lined with mirrors. He swung around, hoping to find an exit door behind him, but there was only a perfect mirror image of the hallway.

Panicked, not knowing which way to turn, he ran forward, legs pumping faster, harder, until they burned. But the corridor lengthened with every passing step, and he cried out in frustration, his footsteps slowing to a shuddering stop.

He bent over, breathless, stifled by the walls which seemed to close in around him.

When he stood up again, Alex saw a man reflected in the mirror, a few years older, a little shorter than himself.

He moved closer, drawn to the man's face, recognising himself in the line of cheek and jaw.

As he drew near, the mirror became a screen, and he saw the man standing in an open doorway with a bag in one hand. He wore a navy suit and a resigned expression, while a small, dark-haired boy held on to his arm and begged him to stay.

Boys don't cry.

Boys don't snivel.

He heard his father's voice as if it were yesterday; the long-forgotten memory of a man he'd barely known and looked so much alike.

Please, Daddy. Don't leave. Mummy will be sad.

He watched the man shrug the boy off—so hard he fell to the floor—and then step away. Alex closed his eyes, trying to block out the sound of the boy's cries.

His fault. It was all his fault.

His eyes snapped open again and he saw his mother's face behind his own, reflected in the mirror a hundred times.

"You're dead," he said. "You're dead and gone."

I'll never be gone.

He lashed out, welcoming the shattered glass and the cuts to his hand. But the sound of shattering glass never came; the mirror was nothing more than dust which fell to the floor like snow as soon as he touched it.

Ashes of the dead, his mother whispered.

Alex jerked back, his feet kicking through piles of dust and ash, desperate to escape the purgatory of his own mind.

But no matter which way he turned, there was another mirror, another memory.

On the bed in his hotel room, his body rose up from the mattress, arms and legs thrashing against the bedclothes as he fought to be free of the nightmare which held him in a stranglehold and wouldn't let go.

As he ran, Alex trailed his fingers along the edge of the wall, feeling it fall away beneath his fingers and crumble to nothing. He ran faster, heels sliding off the edge of the disappearing floor, until his body screamed and his mind shattered.

Then, he was falling, down and down into the abyss where not even he could save himself.

The sound of the lamp crashing onto the floor woke him up.

Alex reared up from the bed, his skin coated with sweat and pale with shock as his body adjusted to the sudden drop in adrenaline. The hotel room was in darkness, the smashed lamp having been the single source of light he'd left burning for a moment such as this.

Sitting there in the semi-darkness with his back to the headboard and the blood pounding in his ears, he felt the old fear rising up again.

Darkness.

He gritted his teeth and whispered the mantra he'd been taught when he was a child.

Stars, moon, movies and meteorites.

None of these things can exist without darkness.

He whispered the words again and again, while he focused on slowing his breathing.

In and out.

In and out.

Gradually, the trembling in his hands began to subside, and he was left feeling intensely cold. He wanted to leave the bed and turn on all the lights, but his body remained frozen, transfixed by a fear that was decades old.

Terrible things wait in the dark, his mother used to tell him. *"Little boys should go to sleep, not get up and walk around. Monsters could catch you.*

He drew his knees up to his chest and wrapped his arms around them, staring wide-eyed into the shadows of the room, and felt for his mobile phone which, mercifully, was still within reach on the bedside table.

Almost three o'clock.

He made a quick calculation in his head and realised it would be around nine o'clock in the evening in Boston.

The phone rang for an agonising second or two, and then Bill Douglas' cheerful voice sounded down the line.

"Bonjour!"

Gregory let go of the constriction in his chest, drawing comfort from the warmth of his friend's greeting.

"Is this a bad time?" he asked, working hard to keep the tremble from his voice. "I don't want to interrupt your jet lag."

"Not at all," Douglas said, and waved away his colleagues, who were gesturing towards the hotel bar. "I was about to head up to my room, as it happens."

Gregory searched his addled mind for some plausible topic of conversation that didn't involve his own neuroses.

"Has there been any progress with Camille?" Douglas asked, helpfully.

Camille. Of course.

"Ah, yes and no. The police have dismissed the psychiatrist—Doctor Gonzalez."

Douglas made a small sound of surprise at the other end of the line.

"Why?"

"Apparently, Camille had some kind of episode and tried to run off. Not only did he fail to report it to the officer leading the investigation, but he failed to mention that she'd made some sounds."

"She spoke?"

"No, she was hysterical—shouting, screaming, but neither the doctor nor the nurse could recall her using any specific words."

Douglas grunted.

"Well, it's still good news. It confirms the medical opinion that her vocal cords are intact. It doesn't completely rule out aphasia, but it makes it very unlikely."

Gregory agreed.

"So, who have they found to take over from Gonzalez?" Douglas asked, innocently.

Gregory smiled into the darkness.

"Go ahead, you can say it."

"I told you so."

"Yes, you did. Does it ever get boring, being right all the time?"

"Not so far. How do you plan to approach it?"

"I spoke with Southmoor, and they're happy that my insurance covers me to take on a few days' private consulting work, so long as I'm back on duty next Wednesday, as planned. I was clear with Inspector Durand about that."

"Your time is limited, but you can still be effective," Douglas said.

"I hope so. I met Camille for the first time, earlier today, and Gonzalez…she was doped up to the max, Bill. She might as well have been in a coma."

The other man swore softly.

"The lacerations to her torso were minor, all things considered. They'll be painful, but not sufficient to justify that level of sedation, and certainly not after three days."

"That's what I thought," Gregory said, shifting the phone to his other ear. "I made some changes to her medication, which was far too high, so we'll see whether she's more communicative when I check on her in the morning."

Douglas made a rumbling sound of approval.

"What did you make of her?" he wondered. "Did you think she was…"

"Faking it?" Gregory finished for him. "I don't think so, but it's too early to say for certain. At first, she seemed to be awake, but kept her eyes closed—"

"Avoidance?"

"Yes, or perhaps another side product of the trauma. She seemed to react physically when I introduced myself; her head jerked, and her facial muscles tensed."

Douglas stepped off the lift and began walking towards his room, which overlooked the Charles River.

"She's responsive, then."

"She was, until her medication seemed to kick in, after which there was nothing," Gregory said, thinking back. "She seemed so withered, so fragile, I'm finding it hard to imagine her as the extrovert she seems to have been before the attack."

"Appearances can be deceptive," Douglas said. "You should know that by now."

Gregory nodded, though his friend couldn't see it.

"I spent some time with Durand, meeting the people who worked alongside her for the past couple of weeks, trying to get some second-hand impressions of her, maybe some information about her life before."

"What about the profiling? Do they still want you to consult on the investigation?"

Muddy water, Gregory thought.

"Yes, but they understand my first duty will now be to Camille—if that's her real name."

"Have they made any progress on that score?" Douglas asked.

"It's still a mystery. Durand's hoping to hear from the bank where Camille set up an account by tomorrow morning, likewise they're hoping the forensics report will come through—but the bureaucracy here is just as slow as any other city in the world, so it's anybody's guess whether that will actually happen."

"Ain't that the truth," Douglas muttered. "Still no word from her family?"

"None," Gregory said, with a touch of sadness. "The papers are still running the story, especially since they got wind that she hasn't spoken. They're calling her the 'Sleeping Beauty', and her attacker 'The Butcher of Beauty'."

"Not all that original," Douglas was bound to say.

"It sounds better in French," Gregory muttered. "Anyway, they're looking into her identity card and driver's licence, to see if that'll lead to something."

"They're thinking forgeries?"

"Yes, and Durand says they've got a few leads, so they'll shake those down tomorrow."

Douglas settled himself on the sofa in his room and toed off a pair of comfortable loafers, leaning back against the chintzy cushions with a sigh.

"What about the fashion police—I mean, people. What were they like?"

Gregory grinned, and had almost forgotten about the surrounding darkness.

"Judging from first impressions? Almost exactly as you'd expect," Gregory said. "I was hoping to find otherwise, and say all those stereotypes are horribly unjustified, but there was an awful lot of white leather, Bill."

Douglas let out a wheezing laugh, which turned into a hacking cough.

"That doesn't sound too good," Alex murmured. "Have you seen a doctor?"

"It's nothing," Bill replied, still coughing as he struggled to uncap a bottle of water. "Just a winter bug, most likely."

The cough seemed to abate, and Gregory relaxed again.

"You should get some rest," he said. "I can give you an update tomorrow."

"I'm fine, I—" Douglas took a long gulp of water to stave off another coughing fit. "It was probably the air conditioning on the plane over. You know what it's like; all kinds of things circulate around the cabin space."

Gregory wasn't convinced, but let it drop for now.

"Get some rest, Bill. Thanks for the chat."

"Anytime, kiddo. Good luck finding the key to Camille Duquette."

After they'd said their goodbyes, Douglas replaced the receiver and turned to check the carriage clock on the mantelpiece in his room. He worked out the time difference and the answer troubled him deeply, because it could mean only one thing.

His boy wasn't sleeping again, and wouldn't tell him why.

CHAPTER 12

By the time Gregory made it across town to the Trente-Six, rain was falling in a steady shower. The blue skies of yesterday had been replaced by thick storm clouds that swept in from the English Channel and threatened to worsen before the day was out. Gregory took a moment to shake the rain from his coat and slick a handful of wet, brown curls out of his eyes, then spotted Procureur Segal approaching him across the expansive entrance foyer. The two men were due to attend a morning briefing with Inspector Durand and Commissaire Caron, who had demanded daily updates on the progress of the investigation.

They shook hands and headed over to the bank of lifts, with Segal exchanging a quick, flirtatious word with a young administration assistant who happened to walk by.

"Juge Bernard has other commitments today, but he's given his authorisation for any additional warrants we may require."

"Durand said you were looking into Camille's identification documents—you believe them to be forgeries?"

Segal nodded.

"Identity fraud is a serious problem, especially if it's done well. Camille seems to have opened a bank account online, which was necessary in order to receive payments from Maison Leroux. We found out that she listed the address of one of the other models—Madeleine Paquet—on her application form, stating that she was renting a room from her."

Gregory's face remained impassive.

"And was she? Renting a room?"

"Not as far as we know, but Durand plans to question her about it again, sometime today. Perhaps they were complicit."

"You're certain the documents are forgeries?"

"There is always a margin for error," Segal replied. "But we do know there's no record of a Camille Duquette matching her description. Often, professional forgers recycle deceased records to create new identities, so we're in the process of cross-checking the death registry. We're following up with the bank, as well, to understand how she could have set up an account without the proper identification checks."

"Assuming you're right, and her identity turns out to be a fake one, then the question still remains: why would she have done it?"

Segal nodded grimly.

"It opens up a huge can of worms," he said. "Not to mention the fact that there are local elections coming up, and the migrant problem has worsened since the border crisis in Calais. If it turns out Camille is an illegal immigrant, it may be that the press will turn against her, and support for her recovery will cease."

Gregory thought of a traumatised young woman, and of the long-term care she might need.

"Let's hope her fate doesn't rest in the hands of public opinion," he muttered.

───────

They were about to step into the lift, when the call came through.

"She's awake, and talking," he said, after a brief discussion with Camille's nurse. "You'll have to excuse me."

Segal broke into a wide grin, which Gregory suspected had a lot to do with the likelihood of police public opinion polls rising by a percentage point or two, now they were a step closer to finding Camille's attacker.

"The Commissaire will be very happy about this," he said, trotting after Gregory as he strode purposefully back towards the main doors. "Give me a moment, Doctor, and I'll accompany you—"

"Absolutely not," Gregory said.

Segal was taken aback, and his neck flushed an ugly shade of red.

"Doctor Gregory, whilst we're grateful to you, I must remind you that you're here as our guest. In the absence of Camille's next of kin, we are responsible for her well-being, and I have a duty to attend."

Gregory stopped, irritated to be wasting precious time explaining matters that were, to him at least, painfully obvious.

"I understand your duty, Procureur," he said. "Unfortunately, you don't appear to understand mine. In taking on the interim responsibility for Camille's psychological wellbeing, my primary duty of care transfers to her, and she is now my first priority. That includes protecting her from overt stressors at a crucial moment in her recovery, which also happens to be in the interests of the investigation, if the goal is to encourage her to talk."

Segal was conflicted between his personal desire to be one of the first to visit their star witness and hear what she had to say, set against his logical understanding that his very presence might prove to be an inhibitor.

Fortunately, logic won out.

"I'd like a report by lunchtime," he snapped, "And, Doctor, if she tells you anything, anything at all—"

"You'll be the first to know," Gregory assured him, and then stepped back outside into the rain.

Gregory took the stairs up to Camille's apartment two at a time.

When the door opened, he was met by the same nurse who'd been in attendance the previous day, a motherly woman by the name of Agnés.

"She's in the living room," she said, darting a quick glance over her shoulder.

"How's she been?"

Agnés looked nervous.

"She's—she's been well behaved. No more attempts to escape or hurt herself, at least."

Gregory caught a note in her voice.

"Has something happened? What did she say, when she spoke to you?"

She took a deep breath.

"She asked who she was, monsieur. When I said to her, 'Aren't you Camille?', she said she didn't know who Camille was, and began to cry."

Gregory thought back to his conversation with Procureur Segal and realised that, if the woman was an illegal immigrant and happened also to be suffering from a bout of temporary amnesia brought on by the trauma, it was small wonder she had no idea who 'Camille' might be.

"She was also confused by her injuries," Agnés said. "She flew into a panic when she touched the bandage on her face, and demanded to see a mirror."

"Did you give her one?"

She shook her head.

"I thought that it would be unwise to distress her any further. I removed the one hanging in the bathroom, too."

He put a reassuring hand on the nurse's shoulder.

"*Merci*, Agnés. You did the right thing. Why don't you make yourself a cup of tea?"

She nodded gratefully, having spent the last forty minutes worrying about whether her young charge would make another escape attempt.

Gregory wasn't sure what to expect when he stepped into the living room, but he was an experienced man, and had been in close confines with the worst specimens of humanity. He could certainly cope with whatever the woman known as Camille Duquette was presently suffering from—amnesia, or *selective* amnesia, as the case may be.

She was sitting by the window watching the rain when he entered, and her long dark hair fell over the bandage on the right side of her face so that, just for a moment, she looked like the living embodiment of one of those moody, black and white photographs they sold from carts on the banks of the Seine.

Girl by the Window, it would probably be called.

She turned at the sound of his footsteps against the plain wood floor and tensed in her chair, hands grasping the arms while she looked over his shoulder, seeking out the nurse.

Gregory stopped dead, held both hands out, palms outfacing, and set his mind to putting her at ease.

"*Bonjour,*" he said, reaching inside his wallet for his photographic driver's licence, which he held up. "*Je m'appelle Docteur Alexandre Gregory—*"

"You're…English?"

Apparently, his accent wasn't as good as he'd previously thought.

"Yes," he said, slipping the card back into his wallet. "I'm a psychologist. I'm here to help."

Her eyes welled up, and they were as he'd previously thought. Large, and very blue.

"I—I can't remember anything."

"You remember how to speak English," he said, with a lopsided smile.

Camille's lips trembled, but she managed a very weak smile, which was followed immediately by a grimace as the action tugged the skin and irritated the wound on her face.

"Do you need something, for the pain?"

She shook her head, and spoke slowly and carefully this time.

"I took some tablets, before."

"If the pain becomes too great, let me know," Gregory said.

She nodded.

"The nurse…she said my name was…Camille."

Before they delved into that particular problem, Gregory gestured towards the sofa, which was set back a short distance from where she had stationed herself beside the window. He hoped it would be far enough away for her to feel safe.

"May I sit, while we talk about it?"

She nodded, but he noticed that she shuffled her chair a little further away—albeit subtly, so as not to offend him.

Which told him something interesting, Gregory thought.

She had empathy.

"Thank you," he said, crossing one leg lightly over the other.

She was studying him intently, which was not an uncommon thing for new patients to do—or new acquaintances, for that matter. Generally, as soon as he told people of his profession, they tended to scrutinize his face, just as Camille was doing, presumably trying to see behind his eyes to find out what he thought about them.

"Have we met before?" she asked.

Gregory smiled.

"Do you think we have?"

"I—I don't know," she said slowly. "Your voice…I think, maybe."

He nodded.

"Yesterday, I came here to visit you with a police inspector called Mathis Durand. You were asleep, but it's possible you might have heard me talking to you."

She nodded, and her fingers began to fiddle with the edge of the soft cotton jumper she wore.

"Why am I here?" she asked, suddenly. "Why are people calling me Camille?"

"Do you have another name?" he asked, very smoothly.

She stared at him, and he could see her struggling to think of it, or anything else at all.

Then, her shoulders slumped.

"I don't know. I don't *know*—"

He heard panic rising, and hurried to extinguish it.

"Do you like tea?" he asked.

She frowned at him.

"What?"

"Tea. Do you like it?"

She looked down at her hands, and then shrugged.

"I suppose…yes."

"Good. I'll make us a cup. Will you be all right here for a moment?"

She nodded dumbly.

He found the nurse, Agnés, flicking through the morning's papers at the tiny breakfast bar in the kitchen. She started to get up when he came into the room, but he shook his head, waving her back into her seat.

"I think we're making progress," he said quietly. "Let's keep the status quo for now."

She nodded, and a couple of minutes later he walked back into the living room with a small wicker tray bearing two steaming cups, a jug of milk and a sugar pot.

He set them down on the coffee table and picked up the jug.

"How do you like it?" he asked, casually.

"Just milk, please," Camille murmured. "No sugar."

He followed her instructions, and handed her the cup.

"So, now we know a couple of things we didn't know before. You like milk in your tea, and you speak very good English."

Gregory gave her an encouraging smile and considered whether to ask an important, but potentially traumatic question. She seemed calm, and fairly relaxed, so he decided to try.

"Do you remember how you were hurt?"

Her face remained entirely blank.

"I have no idea," she said, tearfully. "All I remember is waking up this morning with all these—these bandages, and the nurse won't let me have a mirror, or take them off so I can see—"

Gregory spoke in a calm, even tone. He hadn't forgotten the reports of her becoming volatile, nor the long red scratch on the nurse's arm.

"You suffered an attack," he said. "Your wounds required stitches, but I understand they're healing reasonably well. There was some nerve damage to the skin on your face, and there'll be a scar. I'm sorry."

She raised a hand to touch the bandage covering her right cheek.

"Attack?" she whispered. "Was it a robbery? How did it happen?"

I was hoping you could tell me that.

Gregory was surprised that she hadn't reacted more forcibly to the news that she would have a facial scar for the rest of her life and wondered if it was confirmation that she had no memory of her profession.

If she did, surely she'd have been sorry to lose her means of income, if nothing else.

He reached inside his briefcase, which contained the images of Camille prior to the attack, taken by the photographer Leon. He selected one or two and set them out on the coffee table in front of her, watching her very closely.

"Do you recognise this woman?"

Camille leaned forward to study the photographs, wincing slightly as the bandages on her stomach tugged at her skin.

"She's beautiful," she muttered, with—if he wasn't mistaken—a hint of envy. "I'm sorry, I don't recognise her. Why do you ask?"

Gregory had been listening intently to the inflections in her voice, and watching the emotions flickering across her face. Not once had he seen or heard anything remotely like recognition.

"The woman in these pictures is you," he said, carefully. "They were taken a couple of weeks before your attack."

To say she looked shocked was an understatement.

"*Me*?" she squeaked.

She snatched up the images and held them closer, running her eyes over the pictures of a wildly glamorous woman with a fall of rippling black hair.

"I—I don't believe it," she said tremulously. "Are you sure this is me?"

Gregory almost laughed at her choice of words, which brought the conversation back around to the problem of her identity.

"As far as we know," he said. "Do you remember anything else at all?"

She stared at the photographs for endless seconds, then set them face down on the coffee table and clasped her hands together.

"I don't know her at all—I can't...I can't believe that it's me."

Gregory tried a different approach.

"Do you know anybody by the name of Gabrielle or Armand Leroux?"

If possible, she looked even more confused, so he took out his phone and ran a quick image search until he found one of the couple, taken together at their show the previous night.

"Do you recognise either of these people?"

She took the phone from him and held it carefully in her slim hands, brow furrowing as she tried to capture the thread of a very dim memory.

"I think so," she said, softly. "I think I know this woman."

CHAPTER 13

The rain pattered a gentle, soothing rhythm against the window panes as morning stretched into early afternoon. Gregory and Camille faced one another across the small dining table, their discussion having been interrupted by the arrival of Agnés, who appeared laden with an enormous bowl of soup and Camille's next round of medication. Whether the reduction in dosage had been the deciding factor in allowing her to talk again, they couldn't say; but now, her eyes were much clearer without the fog of unnecessary sedation and she was tucking into the soup with a healthy gusto impeded only by the stitches running so close to her mouth.

"Do you remember how you know Gabrielle Leroux?" Gregory asked, once she'd finished her meal.

Camille set the bowl aside, and shook her head.

"Not exactly," she replied, closing her eyes to try to grasp at the wisp of a memory. "I can't seem to—to capture it."

"Let's try this," Gregory murmured. "Keep your eyes closed, and listen to my voice. Picture Gabrielle, the woman you saw in the picture. Does she have light or dark hair?"

"Very light," she replied, instantly. "I can see it."

"Good. Focus on her hair, and tell me—was the sunlight shining on it?"

"Yes—*no!*" she corrected herself, excitably. "Not the sun. A streetlamp."

Evening time, Gregory scribbled on his notepad.

"Good," he said. "Now, go back to her hair. Can you see it?"

"Yes," she said, folding her arms on the tabletop.

"Tell me what else is around it, Camille. Is there a street, or a house?"

She struggled, her face screwing up tightly, and then she opened her eyes again and he saw misery lurking in their blue-green depths.

"I'm sorry, I can't. It's too hard," she whispered.

"All right," he said gently. "Just one final question, then we'll leave it for now. Is there anything else you remember— anything at all, no matter how small?"

When she tried, there was little more than a blank space; a void where the fabric of her mind should have been. She knew what memories were and why they were important, but found herself unable to recall a single one, and the knowledge of what she lacked was more terrifying than anything else.

And then, amidst the terrifying blankness, came the snapshot of a single image that materialised like the slow shutter of an old-fashioned camera.

"Giverny," she whispered. "I remember Monet's garden."

In another part of the city, Juliette Deschamps gave the cherub-faced toddler another long squeeze, before allowing Anais to wriggle away in search of her grandmother. She watched her small daughter run with arms outstretched towards the woman she thought was her mother.

"Attends, petite!"

Hélène Deschamps scooped Anais up into her arms and gave her a couple of kisses before setting the little girl down again beside a box of toys and books. Juliette watched her daughter root through it, discarding all the new toys she'd bought, until she found a tattered old copy of *The Little Prince*. She was too young to read, but she grasped the book in her chubby hands and carried it over to her grandmother, not sparing a glance for the woman who'd given her life.

Juliette stood up and walked quickly into the kitchen, blinking rapidly against the tears that threatened to fall. She braced herself against the sink, battling a rising tide of emotion she rarely allowed herself to feel. She began to wash the dirty plates, scrubbing at the porcelain with far more force than was necessary, while her treacherous mind wandered back in time, to when she'd found out about Anais three years before.

As a girl of eighteen, she'd been devastated; unprepared for motherhood and unwilling to relinquish the prospect of a glittering career in fashion. Born on a sink estate on the edge of the city to a father whose chronic depression prevented him from holding down a job, and a mother who worked all the hours God sent to make ends meet, she knew what it was to be poor. Growing up, she'd wandered along the Rue Saint Honoré and watched beautiful men and women coming in and out of Chanel or Givenchy and imagined what it might feel like to wear such lovely clothes, and to look so...so *clean*. She'd practised walking along the narrow corridor of their apartment, posing at the end, and walking back again. She'd saved for and studied every edition of *Vogue,* writing down the names of all the fashion houses and the important people who ran them. She had lofty dreams of becoming one of them, and those dreams didn't—*couldn't*—involve babies. Besides, she told herself there was no sense in burdening her family with another mouth to feed.

As for the father...he didn't want the responsibility.

In the end, she made it as far as the waiting room of the abortion clinic before running out, and never going back.

When the baby had been seven months old, and she'd lost every ounce of weight after plumbing the very depths of postnatal despair, she'd landed her first modelling job. At the time, it seemed like fate had stepped in to help, and her star had risen quickly. But the price she paid for success, and for security, was a high one. One she was no longer willing to pay.

"Anais needs new shoes."

Juliette hadn't heard her mother enter the kitchen, and she looked down to find the sink was empty of dishes, and the water cold.

"Of course," she said. "I'll take her—"

"When?" Hélène asked, snidely. "You work all the time—"

So that you don't have to, Maman, she might have said. But she didn't.

"I have a free day coming up, this Sunday. Fashion Week will be over by then, and I don't have any other jobs booked in until next Tuesday."

Her mother sniffed.

"*Jobs?* You wouldn't know the meaning of real work, Juliette. You swan around posing, pouting and showing off your body to all the world…"

She could have argued, Juliette thought. She could have told her mother how exhausting it was, physically and emotionally, and how fickle; she wanted to explain that every piece of food she ate felt like a risk, and every tiny wrinkle a death sentence. She wanted to tell her about the people who saw your vulnerability and tried to exploit it…to…to…

She drew in a shaking breath, while her mother raged on.

"You're not saving any lives, are you?" Hélène was saying. "As for that lingerie campaign, how do you think Anais will feel when she sees *that*? Meanwhile, I wipe her nose and dry her tears…"

Juliette began to dry the dishes on an old tea towel and simply listened, letting the words roll off her back. And, when the dishes were done, she made sure her face wore the same cool, detached expression she was famous for; the one that graced the side of enormous billboards and sold expensive perfumes around the world.

"You offered to look after Anais so that I could go out and work," she reminded her. "I didn't want Papa to worry about money, or you to be so tired, and it was for the best. But now, when I come to visit, my daughter hardly knows me."

She lifted her chin.

"When I make enough money to last, enough to buy a little place where I can study design and Anais can go to school, I'll be coming back for her, Maman. She isn't yours to keep."

Her mother's lip trembled, and she spat out the final words she would ever say to her daughter.

"You're no mother to her, Juliette. It would be better if you forgot all about Anais and went on with your silly life, dressing up in clothes you can't afford."

Juliette stopped with her hand on the doorway and looked back at Hélène with such aching sadness that it shamed her.

"I—I didn't mean…" Hélène started to say she was sorry, but the words stuck in her throat.

"I'll bring some more money on Sunday," Juliette whispered, and then turned to look for Anais, who was happily engaged in the task of emptying and re-filling a magazine rack on the living room floor.

She knelt down and called to the little red-headed girl, throwing her arms wide open.

"*Viens-ici, Anais. Je dois partir, maintenant.*"

Anais looked up, then returned to her task.

Juliette stayed there for an endless moment, eyes burning with unshed tears, then walked across to press a soft kiss to the top of the girl's head.

"*Je t'aime, ma petite*," she whispered, inhaling the scent of her baby skin one last time and promising herself that she'd be back to reclaim her little girl before the week was out.

She had ways—and means.

She let herself out of the apartment, closing the door softly behind her.

CHAPTER 14

The rain had stopped by the time Gregory stepped out of Camille Duquette's apartment building, where he found Inspector Durand leaning against the side of a battered Citröen that looked as though it had survived both world wars. He had a mobile phone in one hand and a half-smoked cigarette hanging from the other, which he raised in greeting.

"How the hell did you manage to squeeze into that gap?" Gregory asked, once Durand had completed his call.

Cars were parked bumper to bumper along the kerb, mere inches separating the Citröen from its neighbours.

"Skill, *mon ami*," Durand replied, and then ground the butt of his cigarette beneath the heel of his shoe. "Jump in, and I'll show you how it's done."

"Do I want to know?" Gregory muttered, but he walked around to the passenger side. "What brings you here, anyway? I thought the meeting with the Commissaire was re-scheduled to four o'clock?"

"It was," Durand agreed, yanking the gearstick into reverse. "I thought it would be a good opportunity to find out how your new patient is getting along, if we travelled together."

In other words, Gregory thought, he wanted to get the scoop ahead of Procureur Segal and Juge Bernard. It made no real difference to him, considering he'd be filing the same report to each of them, but it was an interesting insight into their dynamic—

There was a loud *crunch* of metal as the tail end of the Citröen connected with the bumper of the car behind, followed by a twist of gears as Durand shifted back into first, then another *crunch* as he gave the car in front a dose of the same medicine.

After another couple of bumps, there was enough space for the car to swing out—upon which, it almost connected with a passing cyclist.

"Don't the police over here need to pass a driving test?" Gregory wondered aloud.

When he looked back over his shoulder, he was dumbfounded to find another car already attempting the same manoeuvre in the space they'd just vacated.

"Look around you," Durand said. "No matter how new or expensive the car, every one of them has a few little scratches and bumps. It's a necessary part of living in the city."

Gregory found that hard to believe, and yet, when he scrutinised the metalwork of other passing cars, he was amazed to find it was true.

"Wonder what the insurance premiums are like," he muttered, as they raced towards the river.

"Tell me, did you learn anything useful from your discussion with Camille?"

Gregory glanced briefly at Durand's profile, then back at the road ahead.

"She appears to be stable, for the moment," he replied. "But I think she should continue to be monitored around the clock until we can downgrade her risk assessment, especially following the incident the other day."

Durand nodded.

"At least she's talking now. What of her attacker? Was she able to tell you—"

Both men lurched forward as Durand slammed a foot on the brake, before the bonnet of his car could connect with the back of a delivery scooter.

The inspector rolled down his window and stuck his head out to hurl a few choice insults, then performed an illegal U-turn before speeding off in another direction.

"I can't stand bad drivers," he declared.

"Quite," Gregory muttered, trying to push past the fear of imminent death to remember what he'd been saying.

Oh, yes.

"The woman we're calling 'Camille' appears to be suffering from amnesia. I conducted various tests with her, and it seems she has little or no memory recall prior to waking up this morning. There's been no obvious impact to her motor skills; she's able to walk easily, and could tell me certain likes and dislikes, as well as converse fluently in English—when the level of conversation became more complex, she slipped back into French, so I think it's safe to assume that's her mother tongue."

"That makes it less likely she was an illegal immigrant— unless she'd travelled from a French-speaking country," Durand remarked.

"Possibly. From a clinical perspective, it's reassuring to know that both her short- and long-term memory is operational, although badly impaired."

"You think the amnesia is… genuine?"

Gregory thought back over the hours he'd spent with Camille and gave the question serious consideration.

"There are different types of amnesia," he said. "Retrograde, anterograde…but, given that her scans came back clear, I think she may be suffering from something called 'dissociative amnesia' rather than any kind of brain injury."

Durand grunted.

"What does it mean, 'dissociative'?"

"The disorder is characterised by a patient's inability to recall basic or important memories about themselves— sometimes, enormous blocks of time—usually following a recent trauma. It's called 'dissociative' because, in seeking to block out the memories, the patient's mind is dissociating from those things it finds too stressful or traumatic to process."

Durand thought about it as he executed a sharp left turn and began motoring south-west, towards the 13th Arrondissement.

"If that's the case, Camille would surely wish to block out the trauma of her attack, but why block out memories of her whole life?"

It was a good question, and one that Gregory hoped to answer as soon as possible.

"I don't know, but I'm going to work with her to find out. Perhaps there were things she wished to forget, which seems consistent with the anomalies surrounding her identity. A person doesn't decide to change their name without good reason."

Looking around the darkening streets, Gregory realised they were driving in the opposite direction to the Trente-Six, and had entered an area of Paris he didn't recognise.

"Isn't Police Headquarters on the other side of the river?"

"Yes, but I need to pay one last visit," Durand said. "It shouldn't take long."

He didn't elaborate, so Gregory decided to sit back and enjoy the ride.

"I'm interested to know why Camille started talking today," he murmured. "Why this morning, and not yesterday morning? I cut her medication, but she hadn't consistently been under heavy sedation before then. There were opportunities for her to talk, if she had wanted to."

"She remembers nothing of the attack, then?"

Gregory looked across at the inspector, whose face was cast in shadow.

"Nothing whatsoever, and I didn't press her on it. She was distressed by her inability to remember simple things—

like her name—and I needed to be very careful with her. It's short-sighted to try to force the memories to return because it could put back her recovery."

Durand was ever the optimist.

"All the same, she's talking again. That's what we hoped for—perhaps more will follow."

"I hope so," Gregory said. "For her sake, I hope so too."

The Asian Quarter of Paris was known as Petite Asie or Triangle de Choisy—a triangular district whose boundary lines were the Avenue de Choisy, the Avenue d'Ivry and the Boulevard Masséna in the 13th Arrondissement. It was the main cultural and commercial centre for the Chinese, Cambodian, Laotian and Vietnamese communities in Paris but, unlike 'Chinatown' in London or New York, Gregory could see none of the architecture that would usually serve as a physical embodiment of the area's heritage. Instead, there were a number of seventies high-rise towers known collectively as Les Olympiades and a few Buddhist temples dotted here and there, but that was about it.

Inspector Durand slowed his car to a crawl until he found something that could loosely be described as a parking space, then did his usual 'bump and grind' manoeuvre to edge the Citröen into a space not far from the Olympiades.

"Shall I stay in the car?" Gregory asked, and Durand sized him up with a critical eye.

"No, I think you'll be fine," he said. "But your briefcase will be safer locked in the boot."

Once that task was complete, Durand led the way across a long esplanade running through the middle of the residential towers, leading to a large market area covered by a purpose-built pergola in the middle that was teeming with people.

"In England, the markets close around this time in the afternoon," Gregory remarked. "Here, it seems like they're only just setting up."

They passed tables laden with spices and roasted duck, and his stomach rumbled—a timely reminder that he hadn't eaten in several hours.

"It's an evening market," Durand told him. "There's another one in the car park around the corner."

They continued through the esplanade, inhaling its colourful atmosphere until they reached a road at the end.

"I take it we're here because you've got a lead on a forger," Gregory said. "I thought you'd bring another officer, in case you need to search the place?"

"When I come to Les Olympiades, I come alone," Durand said. "The person you're about to meet is one of my informants, and has been for years. She's seventy-one, has four children and nine grandchildren—and she owns several expensive homes around the city, but prefers to live here, where she feels most comfortable."

He paused meaningfully.

"She also happens to be one of the best forgers in Europe."

"Isn't that the kind of thing the police normally like to prosecute?"

"Ordinarily, yes, but Wendy Li is a special case. She knows everybody, and information tends to flow through her. She shares valuable information with us, and, in exchange, we allow her to carry on with her sideline."

They'd reached the entrance to a small shopping centre, whose colourful neon signage was flickering into life as the sun fell behind the concrete skyline.

"What's Wendy's main line of work?" Gregory asked.

Durand tapped the side of his nose and made directly for the escalator once they were inside the shopping mall. As they rode it up to the next floor, Gregory cast his eye around the shops filled with everything from rice cookers to tiny alarm clocks in the shape of Chairman Mao.

Eventually, they stopped in front of a nail and beauty salon by the name of Lotus Nails.

"Just one thing before we go in, *mon ami*. Wendy likes to tell the future. I figure…it's mostly bullshit, but sometimes, what she says, it comes true."

Gregory smiled.

"Is this the 'valuable information' she gives you, Mathis? I thought the French police had more sophisticated methods of detection."

Durand gave a short laugh.

"We take what we can get," he said, and pushed open the door.

CHAPTER 15

The interior of *Lotus Nails* was long and narrow, with a bank of tables along one side and a bank of hair washing stations along the other, all of which were occupied. A large television set played music videos from the nineties, and Gregory watched a group of women dancing in perfect time to a song he couldn't hear.

"*Où est Wendy*?" Durand enquired of one of the nail technicians, who glanced furtively at the pair of them and then nodded towards the back of the shop.

Even to the most inexperienced eye, the two men looked very out of place in their surroundings, and yet nobody gave them a second glance as they made their way towards the back of the room.

Durand pushed open a door marked 'PRIVÉ', and they stepped inside a break room containing the smallest kitchenette Gregory had ever seen, plus a single armchair upon which a young woman was seated scrolling through social media on her phone. Considering she was nowhere near the age bracket of the woman they were looking for, Gregory assumed Wendy Li wasn't in the office.

But he was wrong.

The girl looked at Durand, then at Gregory—and then, seemingly satisfied, keyed in a swift text message on her phone and vacated the chair.

Durand murmured a word of thanks and tugged the chair away from the wall, so he could access the very corner of the room, whereupon he located the edge of a panel that served as a fake wall and had been wallpapered to match the rest. He applied a bit of pressure and, sure enough, the wall shifted before their very eyes.

Gregory followed Durand into another anteroom, this time covered with shelves and shelves of counterfeit designer goods ranging from handbags to suitcases, watches to ski gear.

But there were no people.

"Through here," Durand said, and pushed back a rail of fake Burberry trench coats to reveal yet another panel cut into the wall.

"It's like a labyrinth," Gregory murmured.

"This is the last one," Durand said, and disappeared behind the coats.

In contrast to the shop front, Wendy Li's private office was supremely high tech.

Gregory had imagined it to be a dark, dank sort of place—worthy of dark deeds, he supposed—but he was surprised to find himself inside a well-lit room painted a sunny shade of yellow, accented with plenty of red and gold. Artificial plants brightened the windowless space and an efficient heating/cooling system kept the ambient temperature steady. Three professional architect's drawing tables had been set up, only two of which were presently occupied: one, by a skinny young man who looked up when they entered, then returned to whatever intricate task he was engaged in, and the other by a tiny, bird-like woman wearing an enormous beehive wig. Her face was a mass of tiny folds and crinkles, offset by sharp brown eyes which measured them both above a pair of half-moon spectacles.

"*Qui c'est*?" she said, in a booming voice which belied her slight frame.

"This is Doctor Gregory. He's helping me with an investigation," Durand said, and left it at that.

"You trust him?"

Durand turned to Gregory with a thoughtful expression.

"For now," he said, with the ghost of a smile.

Wendy let out a peal of laughter and crooked a finger to beckon him forward. Gregory glanced at Durand and raised an eyebrow, receiving a nod from the other man that it was safe to proceed. There were various weapons stashed around the room, but if Wendy wanted to inflict any real harm, she'd have done it already.

Probably.

Gregory approached the tall desk where she was seated, leaving a cautious distance between them. At Southmoor, he'd worked with many patients over the age of sixty and had never found them to be lacking in either the means or inclination to fight, if the mood struck them; consequently, he took a non-discriminatory view of things like old age and proceeded with caution.

Up close, the wrinkles on Wendy Li's face were even more pronounced, and deep crevices fanned out at either side of her eyes, which were presently narrowed as she studied him with a fixed intensity he found vaguely unnerving.

"Hand," she demanded.

"Pardon?"

"Your hand," she said. "Give it to me."

She held out her own, with its network of veins and fine, papery skin, and waited. Gregory thought he heard Durand chuckle beneath his breath, and realised this must be the fortune-telling he had spoken of earlier. There were many more important things they could be doing, but he scarcely had time to voice the thought before she snatched up his right hand and tugged him closer.

As she bent over to study the lines of skin and bone, Gregory watched the beehive wobble precariously atop her head and wondered if it would be impolite to steady it.

"Long life," she pronounced, suddenly.

Was it ridiculous to feel relieved?

"I don't—"

"Quiet," she snapped, and Gregory felt a strong,

unexpected urge to laugh. He wondered what Bill Douglas would say about the interlude, and imagined it would be something along the lines of her being adept at reading minute social 'tells', or body language indicators.

"Shadows," she murmured. "Many shadows."

Gregory's smile faded, and he began to withdraw his hand, but she held it firm.

"Logic… wisdom…" she muttered, tracing a finger over his skin. "But much pain. So much pain."

"I think that's enough."

She looked at him above the semicircles of her glasses.

"You've known fear," she said quietly. "You've faced it before, and will do it again, many times. You hold much pain in your hands, and in your heart; some that is your own and some that belongs to others. Remember, boy, *when I let go of what I am, I become what I might be.*"

Gregory said nothing, and suddenly she dropped his hand and slid from her stool. They watched her cross the room to where she'd left her handbag on a long bench. She began to root around its contents until she let out a small sound of satisfaction and grasped something in her wiry fist.

She turned back to Alex and unfurled her fingers to reveal a small piece of brass shaped like a calabash, with a square hole in the middle. It was inscribed in Mandarin and suspended from a thin piece of leather.

"Take it," she said, and pressed the charm into his hand.

"What is it?" he asked, feeling the weight in his palm. "What does the writing say?"

"Lei Ting talisman," she said. "It asks Leigong, God of Thunder, to expel ghosts and evil spirits. Keep it close to your heart, and she will trouble you no more."

Gregory stared into her dark eyes and felt the small hairs on the back of his neck rise, one by one.

She couldn't know.

She had no way of knowing.

"What makes you think—" He swallowed a sudden constriction in his throat and tried again. "What makes you think I need to ward off evil spirits?"

"Because she's with us, here, in this room," the old woman replied softly.

Durand watched the blood drain from Gregory's face, and stepped forward.

"That's enough ghost stories for today," he said. "We need to know if you've done anything for this woman."

He drew out the stock picture of Camille for her to examine, but Wendy drew on a pair of nitrile gloves before she would touch it.

She might be old, but she was no fool.

"Perhaps I have seen her," she said, after a brief glance. "This is the girl from the papers."

Durand nodded.

"You know her?"

Wendy pursed her lips.

"Anti-terror police were sniffing around here the other week, Mathis. They wanted to know if I created some passports they seized at the border."

Durand gave a light shrug.

"And? Did you?"

She was offended.

"You think I would create such amateurish work?"

Durand held up his hands.

"I had to ask," he said. "What do you want me to do about it?"

"Stop them coming around," she said, perching herself back on her high stool. "It's bad for business."

"The deal is that we won't prosecute you," Durand said mildly. "I never agreed to protect you."

She reached inside her shirt to pull a packet of menthol cigarettes from her bra, where she preferred to keep them.

"I've told you many things, Mathis," she said. "Many important things."

He nodded.

"It's been a fair exchange," he agreed. "Which is why I know you're going to tell us about the woman in that photograph."

She flicked a gold lighter and inhaled deeply, looking between the pair of them.

"If the girl changed her name, her identity, maybe it was for good reason," she said. "Not all who come to me are bad people."

"Maybe so," Gregory said, having recovered himself. "But it isn't just that she can't remember who she *was*. She can't remember who she is *now*. She has no family, nobody to care for her. She's alone without memories to sustain her. I'm trying to help her, not expose her."

Wendy's eyes flicked over his serious face and then she gave a satisfied nod.

"She came to me. Two weeks ago, maybe three."

Durand smiled.

"And? What can you tell us about her?"

In answer, she spoke over her shoulder to the young man who worked silently in the corner of the room. He roused himself and began to search one of the tall filing cabinets set against the back wall.

"My grandson," she supplied. "Young, but he has a good eye."

Presently, he handed a slim file to her and returned to his task.

Wendy flipped open a file with no name, only a passport-sized photograph of Camille Duquette pinned to the front beside the date it was taken.

"I remember faces, not names," she said, answering Gregory's unspoken question. "Camille, aged nineteen."

She chuckled and gave them a knowing look.

"The girl was twenty-four," she said. "But some of them ask to shave off a few years. I obliged her."

The two men exchanged a look of surprise. The woman they'd come to know as Camille Duquette could easily pass for nineteen.

"Can I see?"

Durand made to reach for the file, but Wendy held it out of reach.

"You know I never contaminate my files," she said. "Besides, there isn't much to know about this one. She told me nothing of her past, only what she wanted for her future."

Disappointment was palpable on the air.

"What?" Durand demanded. "You know our agreement—"

"I gave you my word and I've kept it," she shot back. "See for yourself."

She held open the file so they could see, and it was scant on details, telling them no more than they'd already learned from Camille's employment file at Maison Leroux.

"She could not afford the full service," Wendy deigned to tell them. "I told her, she would have no social security number, or tax reference, but I gave her what I could. It was enough for the short term."

They spent a few minutes discussing the finer details, where they learned that Camille's new identity card had come from a legitimate, as yet unassigned batch of stolen government cards, which accounted for their apparent authenticity.

"What about the bank account?"

Wendy shook her head.

"Banks are more difficult than in the old days," she said, ruefully. "I don't dabble there any longer."

Durand made a mental note to ask Camille's bank about how she was able to open an account on the basis of a forged identity card and a borrowed address.

"What was she like?" Gregory asked. "Tell me how you found her."

Wendy smiled slowly.

"Beautiful girl, tortured soul," she said simply. "I couldn't read her palm."

The memory of it seemed to trouble her, because she frowned and stabbed the butt of her cigarette into a small porcelain tray.

"Why not?"

Gregory told himself he didn't believe in any hocus pocus; that it was nothing more than transference and heightened perception, but he still wanted to know why the old woman hadn't been able to use either faculty to gain an insight into the young woman who had come knocking at her door.

"Camille was a girl who knew what she wanted," Wendy said.

She shrugged.

"Confident, a little arrogant, maybe…and, when I looked into her eyes, it was like looking into a mirror. Nothing behind them, only my own reflection."

Gregory thought of his dream the previous evening and shivered again.

"How did she know to come here?" Durand asked. "You don't advertise."

"It's not so hard, if you speak to the right people," she argued. "But…in this case, she came to me by referral."

"Who brought her?"

Wendy didn't answer, and reached for the photograph of Camille again.

"Beautiful girl," she said. "Such a pity, what happened to her. But at least she will have these photographs to console her, in the years to come."

She looked up and her face creased into a knowing smile.

"Leon always had an excellent eye."

CHAPTER 16

It was just shy of four o'clock by the time Inspector Durand swung into the car park at the Trente-Six. After a brief tussle with a Skoda and a Peugeot, the two men made their way up to the conference suite where Commissaire Caron and Procureur Segal awaited them, the Juge having been detained on other matters.

"No surprise there," Durand said in an undertone, as they stepped inside the lift. "It's a wonder he's shown his face, at all."

Gregory cocked his head.

"Oh? I thought Juge Bernard played an important role in the investigation."

Durand scoffed.

"The whole thing is backward," he complained. "Usually, during the early stages, the procureur directs the investigation alongside the police team. A juge is only nominated once the investigation is fully underway and we have a suspect in mind, not before. Even then, the juge's role is mostly deferred to the police team, they are not usually so…"

He waved his hand in the air as he cast around for the English saying.

"*Hands-on,*" he finished.

"Why has it been different this time?"

"Politics—what else?" Durand muttered. "The Leroux supported the Mayor's last electoral campaign, and may not choose to do so again if their wishes are not met. They want this matter about Camille tied up quickly, so their brand is unaffected. Those higher up the chain want no shadow cast upon the Brigade Criminelle, at a time when the world is watching."

Gregory nodded.

"Don't forget, there was no CCTV in the corridors of the hotel when Camille was attacked. How would that look, if it were common knowledge?" Durand said. "There are many private and public interests at stake here."

"But, surely, the Commissaire is independent?"

Durand laughed shortly.

"The city of Paris may have a population of more than two million people, but it's a small world. Juge Bernard happens to be a close personal friend of the Leroux—a coincidence, I'm sure," he muttered, and then added, "Perhaps, we're due another revolution, *mon ami.*"

On that ominous note, they stepped out of the lift and made their way along the corridors of power to provide their report.

"Tell me some good news."

When Commissaire Caron issued her demand from the head of the conference table, Procureur Segal came to attention, unconsciously adjusting his tie in a manner that reminded Gregory uncomfortably of his father.

An Englishman should be smart at all times. Manners and good dress maketh the man.

With the echo of his father's words ringing in his ears, he looked down at his tailored suit and felt a sudden and overwhelming urge to tear it off. The material began to feel tight, like a straitjacket, clinging to his skin so he couldn't breathe, couldn't break free...

Gregory reached for the jug of water with a trembling hand and sloshed some into a glass, drinking thirstily while he brought himself under control. When he set the glass carefully back on the table, he found Durand watching him with open curiosity.

"The team have been following the usual lines of enquiry," Segal was saying. "Mathis?"

Durand turned away from his inspection of Gregory and launched into a summary of the investigation so far.

"Enquiries into CCTV footage have proven fruitless," he said. "Cameras in the foyer of the Hôtel Violette and in the main communal areas showed no suspicious persons that could not be accounted for and, as you already know, there were no cameras on the upper floors other than the penthouse suite—and none in the service stairs or back entrance to the hotel."

Caron could almost see the headlines.

"I presume a press ban has been in operation…to protect the victim and preserve the integrity of the investigation?" she asked.

Segal nodded vigorously.

"Those matters have not been made public, Commissaire."

"Good," she said, folding her hands together. "Good."

Durand cleared his throat before continuing.

"On the orders of Juge Bernard, another search was recently completed of Camille Duquette's room, the hotel grounds and surrounding areas. I'm pleased to say the team recovered her mobile phone, but still no weapon."

"Where did you find the phone?" Gregory asked, actively fighting the stress that threatened to rise up and consume him.

"In the gardens below her hotel room," Durand replied.

"That seems consistent with our theory that the perpetrator fled the scene via the veranda, or the service stairs which back onto the courtyard outside," Segal put in, obviously pleased by the development. "They must have disposed of the mobile phone as they made their escape."

Gregory reserved judgment on that score.

"What did you find on the mobile?" he asked.

"Very little," Durand replied. "It was a burner phone, which is why we made slow progress with the phone companies. They're notoriously hard to trace."

"What about messages or phone calls?" Segal asked.

"Nothing noteworthy," Durand replied, and tapped a finger on the paperwork on the desk in front of him. "I have a full list of transcribed messages here, as well as outgoing and incoming calls. There's nothing pre-dating her employment at Maison Leroux, so we must assume she picked up the phone around the same time she started working for the fashion house."

The others seated around the table spent a moment scanning the printed transcripts of messages recovered from Camille's mobile phone, and found that Durand was absolutely right: there was nothing either noteworthy or sinister, only a collection of mundane text and voicemail messages from the fashion house telling her where to meet, interspersed with the odd friendly message from Madeleine or Juliette, inviting her to some social event or another.

"There are no Facebook, Twitter or any other social media accounts associated with 'Camille Duquette,'" Durand pre-empted the next question. "I've got a tech specialist going over the phone right now, to see if anything else can be salvaged. Maybe something was deleted, before the phone was discarded."

"Good work," Caron said. "If her attacker took the phone, it tells us there must have been something important on it."

Durand nodded. "That's possible, Commissaire."

"More than possible, surely," Segal argued.

"The question is, why would she choose a burner in the first place?" Gregory murmured. "It seems to support a theory that Camille—or whoever she may be—was hiding from something or someone."

"Which brings us back to the question of her identity," Segal said. "How did your enquiries go today?"

"We know that Camille went to one of the best forgers in the business," Durand replied. "Wendy Li identified Camille from her picture and told us she came to see her two weeks ago, shortly after she was offered the position at Maison Leroux."

Both Caron and Segal leaned forward.

"Wendy Li doesn't take odd jobs," Segal pointed out. "How did the girl find her way to that kind of operator?"

"She was referred," Durand replied. "We believe, by the photographer known as Leon."

Caron and Segal reared back again in a simultaneous motion Gregory might have found funny in other circumstances.

"Now, just a moment," the Commissaire said. "Leon is a world-famous photographer, and you're accusing him of having links to the criminal underworld."

Durand nodded cheerfully.

"I took the liberty of running another background check on Monsieur Boucher, and it came back squeaky clean, just as before."

"There you have it—" Segal started to say.

"Which, as any police officer will tell you, is highly unusual for a man of his age and profession," Durand continued smoothly. "I'd expect to see a speeding fine or alcohol-related misdemeanour, at the very least."

"Do you think Leon used Wendy Li's services himself?"

Caron asked. "It would account for the fresh record."

"I think he not only used her services, but he may have worked for her at some stage," Durand replied. "While we were interviewing her, Wendy said that he, 'always had a good eye.'"

Caron held up her hands.

"I can't believe this of Leon Boucher. He has too much to lose."

"Not if this happened before his career took off," Gregory said. "He would have nothing to lose then, and much to gain." He paused, considering the psychology of a man who had grown accustomed to wealth and status. "If what Wendy Li says is true and Leon is connected, that has several implications for your investigation as I'm sure you're well aware. First, and most importantly, it means he knowingly lied by omission. He knew much more about Camille Duquette than he let on, and may be in possession of valuable information about her previous identity and why she sought to change it. Second, his own background is now called into question—and, third, he may have had a motive for seeking to silence Camille."

"You think she may have sought to expose him in some way, or extort money from him?" Segal said.

"It wouldn't be a bad idea to investigate his accounts. Or, all of their accounts, for that matter."

"That will be difficult," Durand muttered, with a meaningful look towards the other two people in the room. "And the people in question are very unlikely to volunteer their accounts."

The room fell silent, then Segal let out a gusty breath.

"Well, in the circumstances, we have no option but to question Leon about these matters," he said, reluctantly.

"I've already set up an appointment with him, first thing tomorrow morning," Durand said, not bothering to hide his relish at the prospect of an interrogation. "It doesn't matter who Leon is, the law applies to everyone."

The other two shuffled uncomfortably, then Caron gave him a stern look.

"That may be so, but I want you to tread carefully, Mathis, not wield a battering ram."

Durand's face was the picture of innocence.

"Would I ever do such a thing?"

CHAPTER 17

"We believe the attacker used a knife."

Back at the Trente-Six, Inspector Durand drew out a series of stark, full-colour pictures taken of Camille Duquette's injuries after she was admitted to hospital, the previous Monday.

"As these images show, and the hospital has confirmed, Camille sustained a single wound to the right side of her face. Thankfully, it wasn't as deep as they initially thought when she was brought in—although the blood loss had been significant. As it turned out, the wound required stitches, there was some nerve damage and there will be an obvious scar, but there's no physical impediment to her speech or other motor functions."

"That's consistent with what I found when we spoke, earlier today," Gregory put in. "She experiences some discomfort chewing and talking because of the proximity of the injury to her mouth, but Camille's lack of communication appears to have a psychological rather than a physical foundation."

Caron nodded.

"And her other wounds?"

"There were a number on her torso, of varying depth, and some defensive wounds on her hands and arms," Durand replied, then reached for a diagram the hospital had provided showing the precise location of each injury. "There were nine wounds on her upper and lower torso, at least fifteen shallow cuts on her left forearm, as well as a single, deeper cut to her right palm."

Gregory closed his eyes briefly, imagining the scene.

An intruder enters the hotel room and overpowers Camille, almost immediately. He grabs her head—maybe her hair—and slams it against the mirrored panel on the wall, smashing the glass and disabling her. As she staggers around and possibly falls to the floor, they produce a weapon, a knife, and raise it high…first, a slicing cut across her face, to mark her forever. Then, they try to inflict a killing blow to the stomach…but she fights back, raising her right hand to try to grasp the weapon, cutting her palm, then raising her left arm to fend off the blows that keep coming…

"The attack must have been interrupted," Gregory said quietly, opening his eyes again. "Whoever did this wanted Camille to be afraid; they wanted to see that look in her eye. They could have come in quietly and made it quick, but instead they were loud and uncontrolled, which risked them being overheard by one of the neighbouring occupants in the other hotel rooms. That tells us something about the attacker's mindset."

"What?" Segal wondered. "That they were amateurish?"

"Possibly," Gregory replied. "It tells us they were angry. Whoever did this felt wronged by Camille; if not her, personally, then what she stood for, who she is. She was offensive to them."

Durand scrubbed a hand over his stubbled face.

"Why her? Of all of them, why her, in particular?"

Gregory simply shook his head.

"Were there any wounds to her feet?" he asked.

Durand nodded, checking the hospital notes laid out in front of him.

"She stood in some of the glass that shattered when she connected with the mirror."

Gregory remembered the soft bandages on Camille's feet the first day he'd visited.

"She's tall—five-ten or thereabouts? To be able to grasp the weapon and put up enough of a fight to keep herself alive, she needed a degree of strength."

"Or be a physical match for her attacker," Durand added.

Gregory met his eyes and nodded again. "Exactly. Is Camille right- or left-handed?"

They looked amongst themselves, and he made a note to find out the answer at their next appointment.

"Looking at the angle of the knife wounds to her torso area, it suggests her attacker was left-handed," Segal remarked, with just the right balance between smugness and self-deprecation to set Durand's teeth on edge.

"Unless they used a back-handed stroke," Gregory said mildly, taking the wind out of his sails. "Have there been any developments on the forensics?"

Segal's face fell again.

"Yes, and it's a wash-out," he said. "The preliminary report came through about an hour ago, and the upshot is, there were no obvious traces of 'alien' DNA on Camille's person, the mirrored panel or any of the more obvious areas where contact may have occurred, such as the door or the window. No fingerprints that haven't already been accounted for, either. The team are still sifting through the remaining samples taken from the room but there are countless old traces from previous hotel occupants…it's a forensic nightmare."

It might have been disappointing, but it wasn't unusual for there to be no useable samples—in fact, Gregory was more used to working on cases where there was little or no physical evidence, and the police team needed alternative means to trace the mind responsible for perpetrating the crime.

"No latex or nitrile?" he asked.

It was possible the perpetrator wore gloves, which wouldn't help the police team to trace the perpetrator via ordinary methods, but it might help him to understand whether they sought an organised or a disorganised mind.

"Not so far," Durand replied. "But it's early days."

Commissaire Caron sighed deeply and leaned back in her chair, rolling her neck around to stretch out the knots that had developed over the last few days.

"Doctor Gregory, as you can see, we're no further forward than we were before—"

"Respectfully, Commissaire, I disagree," he interjected. "Twenty-four hours ago, we wondered whether Camille Duquette would ever speak again, but now she has. We didn't know why her identity was a mystery, but now we know she *wanted* it to be that way—although we still don't know why. Perhaps the interview with Leon will help shed light on that tomorrow."

Caron nodded.

"Tell me then, Doctor, what's your professional opinion of the woman we continue to call Camille Duquette?"

"As a clinician or as a profiler?"

"Both."

Gregory ran a hand through his hair and let it fall away again.

"I spent several hours examining Camille this morning, talking to her, checking her motor function, long- and short-term memory capacity," he said. "It's all there, in my report. But, if I were to summarise it, I'd say that the woman I met this morning bears no resemblance to the woman we've heard about from those who spent time with her during the past few weeks. I saw no hint of over-confidence verging on arrogance—but subdued behaviour could be attributable to the trauma and her present amnesia."

"You think the amnesia is real?" Segal asked.

"It appears very genuine," Gregory replied. "But she was able to recall small details about her preferences—whether she liked tea—and she had a memory of Monet's Garden at Giverny. That may, or may not, be significant."

The procureur made a note to follow it up.

"As I said before, I believe her present condition to be dissociative amnesia—formerly known as hysterical amnesia—which usually sets in following severe trauma. However, it's an extremely rare condition, made even more unusual by the fact it isn't localised."

"What do you mean?"

Gregory turned to Durand.

"I mean that it isn't just a case of Camille not remembering the events immediately surrounding and prior to her attack, it's a case of her not remembering any details of her life whatsoever, including basic facts such as her name or age."

Segal snorted.

"She's having you on, *mon ami*. For whatever reason, she went to Wendy Li to change her identity and her past caught up with her, that's all. When she came around at the hospital, she knew she would be found out, and she's buying time."

Gregory thought back to the woman he'd spoken to that morning and did the only thing any educated person would do—he doubted himself.

He thought back over every small gesture, every look, every word, and asked himself whether he had been duped. His profession relied in large part on interpreting subjective experiences reported by the patient, taking into account their surrounding circumstances. Therefore, the possibility of being misled was always a real one, and something he never overlooked in his daily work at Southmoor.

On the other hand, he had a certain capacity for stepping behind the veil and into the skin of those he met, walking around their minds as though he were walking in their shoes, and he hadn't been fooled yet.

"Her reactions seemed genuine," Gregory reiterated. "That doesn't preclude the possibility that her mind has succumbed to amnesia as a defence mechanism of some kind; the two aren't mutually exclusive."

"Time will tell, Doctor. In the meantime, we have a victim with no identity, no suspect and no leads."

Gregory smiled slightly, thinking of all the times he and Bill Douglas had argued over the diagnosis and prognosis of a patient.

Too many to count.

"One thing we may be able to agree on is that the factual evidence and the pathological traits Camille has displayed both seem to point towards the same thing, which is that she knew her assailant, or who they represented. It's far more likely her mind would have blocked out all events prior to the attack if those memories were already unwanted."

"A prior relationship, perhaps?" Durand wondered. "There had been signs of sexual activity, although not recent."

Caron had been listening with interest.

"What about Missing Persons reports?" she asked. "Have there been any developments on that score?"

Durand stretched his arms above his head, revealing two perfectly circular sweat patches.

"Nobody's made a report matching Camille's description," he replied. "And none of the people who have come forward fit the bill."

"Let's go over them again," Segal surprised them all by saying. "We've got little enough as it is, so let's make doubly sure we haven't let something slip through the net."

Whether his proactive attitude was intended to impress the Commissaire or was a genuine display of judicious policing, Gregory couldn't tell, but it was a step in the right direction, and he took the opportunity to capitalise on the procureur's sudden show of interest.

"I understand Camille listed Madeleine Paquet's address on her bank account application form," he said. "Did she keep the rest of her belongings at that address? There were very few items found at the hotel room."

Segal looked mildly embarrassed, the thought never having occurred to him.

But it had occurred to Inspector Durand.

"I paid Mademoiselle Paquet a visit yesterday morning. Nice girl, nice place," he added, with a knowing look for Gregory. "She had in her possession a small holdall belonging to Camille, containing some clothing and toiletries, but very little else. I've sent them to the lab, for testing."

As the room began to disperse, a thought occurred to Gregory. "Was there any jewellery in the holdall?" he asked. "A necklace, for example?"

Durand smiled.

"There was a cheap silver locket, containing a picture of a little girl."

"Hers?"

"Who knows, until the results come back, or she tells us otherwise? But, if we should ask Juliette Deschamps, I wonder if it may turn out to be hers."

Gregory thought again of the woman he'd met that morning. Her manner had been so honest, and yet it was likely she'd stolen that necklace from one of her fellow models, then lied about it.

Doubts crept in again, this time much stronger than before.

CHAPTER 18

Later, as night fell over the city, Juliette Deschamps took a taxi from her mother's house back into the city centre, intending to meet up with Leon, or some of the other people she called friends. The interlude with her family had been a painful one, stirring up emotions she spent most days trying to suppress, and had left her feeling lonely and in need of solace. But, as the bright lights of the city centre approached, she found she didn't want to socialise after all and walked back to the studio apartment she rented on the top floor of a mansion block—not far from the safe house where Camille Duquette was staying, in the 7th Arrondissement near to the Eiffel Tower.

It was a poky place and smelled of damp, but Juliette didn't need anything fancy; not when she was working so hard to save money for the future. It was only somewhere to sleep and, if she ever grew lonely or sad, she could look out of her window at the Tower and feel uplifted. Its magnificence was something she remembered first seeing when she was a child, no bigger than Anais was now...

Anais.

Juliette brought a hand to her stomach, which was flat and unlined despite the baby that had once grown there. It wasn't unheard of, for catwalk models to have babies—only, they usually had them once their name was established and they could afford time off, without the risk of being forgotten in an industry where people were replaceable. Consequently, most of the models she knew were childless; some even actively against having children at all, being firmly of the opinion it would ruin their blossoming careers. She supposed they were right to be wary; outwardly, things seemed to be getting better, with the fashion industry hiring curvier models in an effort to be politically correct in the age of spin. But inwardly…

Things hadn't changed all that much, and "perfection" was still their stock in trade. Thanks to genes and good fortune, Juliette was naturally a very slim person, but there were some who went to extreme measures never to gain weight, putting their health at risk in the process. Against that backdrop, the idea that a fashion house would hire a girl who'd recently had a baby—one who had yet to make her mark as one of the profession's rising stars—had seemed a bridge too far when Anais was first born.

And so, she simply hadn't mentioned it.

Just then, a group of young men rounded the corner, laughing and jostling each other as they made their way out for the evening. Juliette ducked her head, hoping they would pass by without comment. On another night, she would have stalked past them with her head held high, uncaring of what was said or by whom. But tonight, her reserves were low, and she couldn't seem to muster the strength to deal with an unwanted exchange.

"Eh! Salut, belle femme! C'est quoi cette Barbie?"

She folded her arms and quickened her pace, heels clicking a staccato rhythm against the pavement.

"*Casse-toi,*" she muttered, and ran across the street as they jeered, calling out lewd suggestions she wouldn't have repeated in polite company.

Once their cries grew distant, tears began to fall. She scrubbed them away with an angry hand, annoyed with them—and herself. It was hardly the first time she'd dealt with unwanted attention, was it? Since the age of thirteen, she'd been aware of eyes following her down the street, or into school. She hadn't looked like most girls her age, much as she'd tried to hide it, and as she'd grown older the situation had become more pronounced and the advances more open.

Until, one day, she'd made a decision that had changed her life.

She'd been a fool, back then. A young, stupid fool who'd believed in things like love and marriage, and happily ever after. The silly fairy tales she'd read at bedtime, to escape the harsher reality she found at home.

But, as God was her witness, she swore that Anais would never know what it was to feel hunger or fear. She wouldn't know humiliation or degradation…

It would be a bright world of opportunity for Anais.

She'd make sure of it.

Juliette reached for her door key, pausing for a moment to admire the lights blazing along the long, rusted columns of the Eiffel Tower which rose up over the surrounding rooftops. She stayed there until the lights were extinguished again, not minding when a slight drizzle began to fall, coating her skin in a layer of fine moisture.

"*La vie est belle,*" she murmured.

She reached to put her key in the lock but found the outer door already ajar. That wasn't unusual—it wasn't the first time one of her neighbours had forgotten to close it properly, or had deliberately left it open while they dashed to the shop for some milk or cigarettes.

Juliette stepped into the dim hallway and, after a moment's thought, left the outer door ajar again. It might be old Monsieur Gerard who had gone out in search of tobacco, and he routinely forgot to take a key. Then, she checked her post box, which was full of letters that had been delivered whilst she'd been staying at hotels around the city.

"*Alors,*" she murmured, and began rifling through the stack of mail as she climbed the narrow, spiral stairs to the top floor.

Payment remittance notice from Maison Leroux.

Monthly service charge invoice from the caretaker of the building.

Agency fees invoice from her modelling agent.

As she reached the third floor, she could no longer read the letters because the solitary light dangling from the ceiling had blown. That, too, was not unusual; she might have paid a monthly service charge for the maintenance of the building, but she couldn't see how the investment was spent. The plasterwork on the walls was crumbling away, and the paintwork badly scuffed, not having been replenished for at least a decade. The ancient cast iron radiators on each landing hadn't worked for months and consequently the air was always chilly, made even more so by the gaps in the wooden sash windows that were rotting away from lack of upkeep. With all these oversights, it was hardly likely the caretaker would trouble himself to replace a bulb.

If she had time before the shoot the next day, she'd replace it herself.

As she passed beneath the dangling shade, she heard a *crunch* as her boots met with fragments of broken glass that lay shattered on the stone floor. Assuming that the bulb hadn't been fitted correctly and must have fallen from the ceiling, Juliette told herself that was the final straw and she'd make a complaint first thing in the morning. There were children living in the building as well as the elderly, and it might have caused an injury.

Fuelled by righteous indignation, she jogged the remaining flight up to the top floor, intending to seek out a dustpan and brush. She didn't bother to close the door properly behind her, never suspecting that she was not alone, or that anyone had been waiting for her to return home.

She didn't see the figure until they were almost upon her and, by then, it was too late.

Much too late.

And, when she knew the end was near, Juliette thought only of one thing.

Anais.

Eva Bisset watched the drizzle collect on her skin, holding her hands up to the night air, blinking as it fell into her eyes and settled on her lashes. People passed by on the street below, their footsteps clattering against the wet paving stones as they hurried to seek shelter before the rain grew heavier. She watched their blurred bodies moving back and forth and envied their freedom, wondering what that would be like.

She began to sing a lullaby, just a few bars of something she'd once heard, then rubbed her temple to soothe the throbbing headache that pounded around her skull.

CHAPTER 19

Gregory heard her voice as soon as he entered the hotel.

The sad, soft strains of *My Funny Valentine* filled the ground floor of the Hôtel d'Aubusson and he paused to listen for a while, letting the music wrap itself around him like a cocoon. It was coming from the direction of the Café Laurent, a venue which had attracted many of the jazz greats over the years and happened to be the hotel's bar, connected by an open passage to the foyer.

It was a little after eight o'clock—early by Parisian standards—but already a crowd had gathered beside the bar to listen, some of them regulars who lived thereabouts, others guests of the hotel like himself.

He didn't intend to join them.

He shouldn't.

And yet, he found himself crossing the foyer, drawn inexorably to the siren's call.

When he stepped into the bar area, he saw that Margot, or *Madeleine*, was sitting on a stool beside a pianist and a saxophonist, though she needed little accompaniment to capture the audience, who gazed up at her from plush leather seats while they nibbled caviar and macarons from small silver platters. It was a very different setting to the one she'd graced two nights before, but the feeling was just the same, and hit him just as hard.

Alex kept to the shadows at the back of the room and braced a hand on the wall, telling himself that, in another minute, he'd leave.

Just as soon as the song finished.

But he stayed there as one song melted into another, a lump rising to his throat as she sang the blues. People came and went, some of them casting an interested eye over the tall, dark-haired man with bold green eyes that were only for her.

He knew he should leave; that's what Doctor Gregory would do.

But what would Alex do?

He raised a hand to loosen the tie at his neck, yanking it from his body with short, sharp movements. Next, he shrugged out of his jacket and folded back the cuffs of his white shirt, as if loosening his clothes would transform him from the man he told himself to be, to the man he really was.

Very deliberately, he stepped out of the shadows and began to weave his way through the tables, keeping his eyes on the stage until he found a spare seat, where he could listen to the whole set.

He saw her eyes widen as she recognised him, heard the tiny falter in her voice, and then…

Then, he saw her smile.

"Can I buy you a drink?"

She had a break at eight-thirty, and he rose to hold out a chair as she approached his table.

"Water will be fine."

White-coated waiters were circulating the room and Gregory placed her order, alongside a Negroni for himself.

"You sing beautifully," he said, when they were alone again. "But I've told you that, already."

A smile hovered around her lips.

"Thank you," she murmured. "If it paid a little more, I'd much rather spend my life doing this than working in fashion."

"You don't like it?"

Soft, shaded lights cast her face in shadow as she looked away from his eyes, which were altogether too probing.

"It pays the bills," she said carefully. "Lots of women—and men, too—would love to be in my shoes."

He thought of the adverts he'd seen in shop windows bearing her face and thought that she was right; there would be some who looked on and envied her life, or what they imagined it to be.

"But not you," he said quietly, and she looked up again.

"No, not really," she admitted. "It's—"

The waiter arrived with their drinks and the conversation was interrupted for a moment while he laid out little trays of nuts and olives, then exchanged a word with Madeleine to compliment her singing. Gregory watched her body language throughout, noting the smile that didn't quite reach her eyes, and the way her mouth immediately turned down as soon as the social pleasantries were complete.

"You give a very good impression," he remarked.

"Of what?"

"Happiness," he said simply. "You can flick it on like a switch, and then turn it off again just as easily. That's quite a skill."

She selected an olive and popped it in her mouth, chewing idly.

"I could say the same of you," she replied. "I've seen you three times now, and each time it feels like I'm meeting a different man."

Was it so obvious? he wondered. *Was it so brazen, the fact he didn't truly know himself, or the man he'd fashioned from the leftover scraps of the boy he'd once been?*

"What makes you say that?"

He was stalling for time—curious, he supposed, to see if there might be another person as perceptive as himself. It was a lonely road, the path he'd chosen to take, and a hard one. How could he hope to seek out the darkness in other people's souls, to help them to heal, and not be burned during the process? With every new case, some of their torment crept into his heart and made a home there, so he could no longer be certain of where they ended, and he began.

"At the club, you were warm and playful, with plenty to say about music and art," she began. "I thought…I was looking forward to seeing you again. But then, when you turned up at the reconstruction yesterday, I saw a different side. You were aloof, distant. As if you didn't want to know me."

"You're a witness in the case," he said.

"Even so."

"I shouldn't be sitting here with you, now," he added, so they were both absolutely clear on where things stood. No matter how flippant Inspector Durand might have been the previous day, he and his superiors wouldn't take kindly to their criminal profiler becoming romantically entangled with a material witness in their investigation—one who could still, conceivably, be a suspect.

But Madeleine was right about one thing.

She wasn't seated beside Doctor Gregory, the clinician. She was with Alex, who was a very different man entirely.

"How long do you have left, before your next set begins?" he asked softly.

She read the unspoken question in his eyes.

"Long enough," she replied.

He rose from the table and held out his hand.

After a moment's hesitation, she took it.

CHAPTER 20

The ground was hard and brittle beneath his feet, tearing the soles of his feet as he stumbled through the darkness towards the open doorway.

Where do you think you're going?

"I'm leaving," he said. "I'm never coming back."

You can never leave.

He walked a little faster, feeling the shards of broken glass nick his skin and not caring, so long as he made it to the doorway before the light was extinguished.

Stars, moon, movies and meteorites.

Stars, moon, movies and meteorites.

And monsters, his mother added. *Terrible things wait in the dark for bad boys like you.*

The door started to close, and he began to run, crying out as the glass penetrated his skin, reaching blindly for the light before it was too late.

He burst through the doorway and felt the warmth of the sun against his skin, blinding him at first, but then the world came into focus again and he found himself standing in a beautiful summer garden. Flowers bloomed everywhere, their petals creating a patchwork of colour around an enormous lily pond, bordered by weeping willows.

The ground was no longer jagged, but soft and springy, the grass thick and green beneath his feet. Alex took a step closer to the pond, ducking beneath the hanging vines of the willow tree so he was shaded beneath its fold.

But he was not alone.

A woman was seated there, her long dark hair falling in rippling waves across one side of her face while she watched a pair of swans gliding on the water.

"Camille?"

She continued to look out at the water.

"What's your name?" he asked. "Who are you?"

She turned to look at him then and, as her hair fell away, he saw blood running from a gaping wound on the right side of her face, and even more seeping through the silk pyjamas she wore.

I'm you, she said. *I'm everybody and nobody.*

When he looked down, there was a deep cut on his right palm.

He stumbled away, pushing through the long branches and back out into the sunlight. On the other side of the pond, there stood a beautiful blonde girl. She waved to him, and beckoned him towards her, but there was no bridge to span the distance, nor any boat to carry him across.

And he couldn't swim, for his arms were bound tightly inside the straitjacket he wore like a second skin.

———————————

Alex awoke with a shout.

Sometime during the night Madeleine had turned the lights out, and he found himself shrouded in darkness, shivering so hard his teeth chattered.

"Alex?"

The light came on again and Madeleine sat up, her body unashamedly naked in the glow of the lamp.

"Just—just a nightmare. It's nothing."

She raised a hand to his head, but he jerked away. It had been a long time since he'd shared a moment of vulnerability with anyone, especially where he was the one receiving comfort, rather than dishing it out.

"You look as if you'd seen a ghost," she said, drawing the covers a little higher to stay warm against the cold draught that seemed to emanate from him. "What can I do?"

"Nothing," he said bleakly. "There's nothing you can do. I'm sorry to have woken you up."

"Don't be silly," she muttered. "It doesn't matter. I don't have any work tomorrow, anyway. I want to help you, if I can."

Doctor Gregory returned, along with his logic. "You can help me by telling me why Camille Duquette put your address down as a contact on her bank application," he said.

She was taken aback.

"I—should I be talking to you about this?"

"It seems a little late for circumspection," he said. "None

of this is admissible, anyway, but I want to know. Call it curiosity."

She flopped back against the headboard and reached for the bottle of water sitting on the bedside table.

"When I met Camille for the first time at the Leroux party a couple of weeks ago, she told me she was looking for a new place to stay. I assumed she'd had a bust-up with an ex-boyfriend or she'd moved from another city."

"You didn't ask?"

"No, I didn't. Camille was very private about her past, and I felt it polite not to enquire in case there had been a bereavement or something of that kind."

"She didn't give you any details?"

"No. Like I say, we were only briefly introduced. I offered her a place to stay, temporarily, while we were working together."

"Very trusting," he remarked, and she turned to look at him.

"Yes," she muttered. "I have a spare room at my apartment, and… I didn't want to be alone."

She swallowed and turned away from him to take a long gulp of water.

"How did you find her, as a house guest?"

"Unobtrusive," she replied. "Tidy…but unpredictable."

"What do you mean?"

"She only stayed for a few days before we were carted off to the hotel, and she was hardly around," Madeleine elaborated. "She never came home at night, so I assume she was sleeping elsewhere, either with family or a boyfriend. I told the police all of this."

But Gregory wasn't so interested in that.

"You said she was *unpredictable*. What do you mean by that?"

She took another sip of water.

"I mean, she could be moody. One minute, she was all smiles, the next…totally different. And she liked to rifle through my things."

"You caught her?"

Madeleine shook her head.

"No, but I came home a couple of times to find my clothes had been left out on the bed or moved around. It was odd, because she was generally very tidy, as I say."

Gregory filed away the information for later.

"Did you like her?"

"I…I didn't *dislike* her," she said. "I suppose, to be honest, she put me on edge. She was very ambitious, and fashion was all she talked about, which bored me. All the same, I was sorry to see what had happened, and I hope she's doing better now. I'd like to visit her sometime, when the police say it's all right."

Gregory nodded.

"Do you have any idea who might want to hurt her?"

She looked away again, and drew her knees up to her chest. It made him want to reach out and draw her closer, to comfort whatever sadness had touched her heart.

But he didn't.

"Was there a man?" he asked.

She leaned her head back against the pillows and laughed.

"There's always a man," she said bitterly. "In fact, there's usually more than one."

"Madeleine—"

"You hardly know me," she said suddenly. "And I hardly know you. Let me give you a crash course, *Doctor Gregory*. My name is Madeleine Margot Paquet, and I look a certain way. It hasn't always brought me joy, or success; sometimes, it's brought me trouble. As for the glamorous world of fashion…it's as bad as the film world. Maybe worse, because nobody has started a movement for women's rights. You think Gabrielle runs Maison Leroux? *Son mari est un souteneur.*"

Gregory didn't catch the last sentence, but it was spoken with such vitriol, he knew it must have been something derogatory. There was no time to question it, because Madeleine was already rolling off the bed to search for her clothes.

"You don't have to go. I'm sorry about the Spanish Inquisition."

She sent him a confused look.

"*Quoi?*"

Monty Python clearly wasn't a part of the English syllabus in France.

"Never mind. I meant, I'm sorry for asking you all those questions."

She hovered, dress in hand.

"You don't know my world," she said eventually. "I haven't always sung songs at nice jazz cafés."

"You don't know mine," he shot back. "And I've never sung songs, except in the shower."

That brought a smile to her lips and, as they looked at one another, he realised he'd forgotten all about the nightmare.

CHAPTER 21

Saturday 28th September

It was shortly after eight when Thierry Lebrun arrived outside Juliette Deschamps' apartment building. As a runner for Leon, he'd worked with her a couple of times and knew her to be one of the very best in the business, part of a new wave of models with a 'classic' look that harkened back to images of women in the eighties and nineties. She dressed impeccably, her skin was flawless, and she gave every impression of being a woman at the top of her game—she had never been late for work before.

Which is why he was surprised to find himself outside a second-rate mansion block on a dingy street in the 7th Arrondissement, trying to wake her up.

He checked the names printed on a laminated card outside the main door and, sure enough, hers was listed as the sole resident on the fourth floor.

He rubbed his cold hands together, blew some hot air on them, then pressed the buzzer again.

There was no answer, and he hopped from one foot to the other, hugging himself as an icy blast of wind rushed along the narrow street, stirring up the litter that had been discarded sometime during the night.

"*Allons*," he muttered.

He pressed the buzzer again and held his finger there for long seconds.

Still no answer.

He tried her mobile phone, but the number rang out several times and he chewed his lip, wondering what to do for the best. It wouldn't have been the first time he'd been called upon to drag a model out of bed after a heavy session the night before, but he couldn't perform miracles and there were plenty of others waiting to take her place—and he was getting cold. The coat he wore might have been the height of fashion, but it wasn't built to withstand much more than a mild breeze.

After another unsuccessful attempt at the buzzer, Thierry was about to give up when some instinct compelled him to try the door.

It opened easily.

Shaking his head at the lack of security, he stepped into a dim hallway with a bare stone floor. A bank of post boxes was set against one wall and a narrow staircase led to the upper floors. There was no lift, so he grasped the bannister and began the ascent, wishing he wasn't so unfit. His feet crunched against a small pile of broken glass as he reached the third floor, and he glanced up at the light fitting with its filthy cream shade, thinking once again that it was surprising somebody of Juliette's means should choose to live in such a place when others of her calibre were in swanky penthouses overlooking the river.

He was perspiring by the time he reached the top floor, and he ducked his head beneath a low-hanging beam to knock loudly on the single, shabby-looking door bearing her name.

"Juliette!"

There was no answer still, and he pressed an ear to the wood, straining to hear any sounds of life from within.

Just then, he heard footsteps approaching from the floor below. The stairs creaked beneath the weight of an old man, who leaned heavily on the bannister as he dragged himself up the final flight. He introduced himself as Monsieur Gerard, her nearest neighbour, and there ensued a brief discussion where Thierry learned that Juliette had come home sometime around seven-thirty the previous day—the old man had heard her floorboards creaking above his head, and then some crashing around. He'd hammered a broom against the ceiling and the noise had stopped, then she'd gone out again a few minutes later—and seemed to have been in a hurry judging by the speed she'd clattered down the stairwell.

Thierry's heart fell, because, if Juliette wasn't at home, he had no idea where else she could be.

With a boyfriend or somebody she'd met the night before?

It seemed unlikely; of all the different characters he met in the industry, Juliette Deschamps had never given the impression of being remotely interested in the opposite sex—or her own, for that matter. Nor had she ever been so unprofessional as to miss the beginning of an important shoot and place her reputation in jeopardy.

He thanked the old man and was turning to leave when he spotted the blood.

Just a tiny trail, nothing more than a couple of spots on the stone floor, but enough to send his heart thumping against the wall of his chest.

"*Appelle le gardien,*" he said shakily, and while the old man bustled off to find the caretaker, he called the police.

When Gregory arrived at the scene less than an hour later, he spotted Inspector Durand's Citröen parked on the kerb outside Juliette's apartment, next to a nondescript white van belonging to the city's coroner and a couple of white and blue squad cars. A pair of officers were engaged in the important task of setting up a cordon to keep press hounds and rubberneckers at bay, having anticipated that the level of morbid fascination would reach a fever pitch, once the news broke that a second catwalk model had been attacked.

And this time, her killer hadn't been interrupted.

Gregory scrawled his name in the logbook and slipped on some protective overalls before he was escorted inside the building, which wasn't much to look at from the outside, but was somehow even less impressive on the inside. He was met with a stale odour of mildew mingled with a potent aftershave he attributed immediately to the procureur, who must have passed through the dank hallway a short time before.

"Monsieur?"

He followed the young police officer up a narrow flight of stone stairs which had already been coated in a fine layer of protective plastic. His eyes roamed the floor and the walls, not looking for anything specific except, perhaps, the shadow of a criminal.

He found the first one as they reached the third-floor landing, where a yellow forensic marker had been placed beside what remained of a broken bulb. Gregory stopped to look down at the scattered fragments of glass and filament, then up at the light fixture, where the remains of the metal bayonet cap could still be seen. A crime scene investigator—an officer of the *Police Technique et Scientifique*—was crouched on all fours beside the skirting board, her polypropylene suit rustling as she brushed tiny slivers of glass into an evidence bag. She looked up from behind a hooded mask and he met her eyes, before continuing upward, where his next nightmare awaited him in the flesh.

Gregory would never forget the sight of Juliette Deschamps.

He had seen many things in his time as a clinician and

was not afraid of the sight of blood; an ability to withstand a certain level of trauma was a prerequisite for the work he did each day, and his tolerance had been tested many times before, in the saddest of circumstances.

But this felt different, somehow.

Her killer had displayed an exceptional level of cruelty; a disregard for humanity he seldom came across, even at Southmoor, where 'humanity' was a fluid term.

"How long has she been dead?" he asked quietly.

Durand battled his own emotions and the strong urge for a cigarette.

"The examiner thinks at least twelve hours," he said.

There was a stifling odour of blood lingering on the air in the small studio, mingling with something worse that reminded him of over-ripe fruit. Post-mortem lividity had set in, turning the visible parts of Juliette's skin a translucent grey as whatever blood that remained succumbed to gravity and settled on the underside of her body. Were it not for the congealed blood caking her hair, and the ugly, gaping wounds on her skin, she might have been a mannequin— beautiful, even in death.

"The examiner found a cut to the right side of her face, in exactly the same place as Camille's."

Juge Bernard delivered the update with a sombre expression, and was joined by Procureur Segal, who had been engaged in the task of liaising with the senior forensic technician.

"There were lacerations to the stomach and torso as well," he said. "It's very similar to what happened before."

"It must have been the same man," Durand agreed. "There are too many similarities to overlook; the victim type, the fact she was a witness, not to mention the injuries…it's too much of a coincidence, especially since the precise details of Camille's wounds were not made public. That reduces the likelihood of there being a copycat."

Gregory stepped closer to Juliette's body, which lay in a perfect circle of blood. Her life force had pumped from her body onto a cheap circular rug she'd laid out to brighten the room, which consisted of a sofa-bed, two large wardrobes and a tiny kitchenette, with a separate en-suite bathroom. As he approached, he saw what the examiner had seen: ragged tears to her clothing and skin, and a series of lancing blows to her forearms which must have been sustained as she fended off further blows, in an ill-fated effort to survive.

He turned back to gauge the distance between the door and the place where she'd fallen, estimating it to be no more than ten paces. Blood was spattered across the magnolia walls and on the bare floorboards in long, thin arcs, roughly forming a perimeter around her body.

But there was nothing immediately beside the door.

"The intruder gained access to the apartment first," he surmised. "They didn't attack straight away, or there'd have been blood on the walls beside the door, over there."

"It's the same as before," Bernard remarked. "The perpetrator managed to get inside Camille's hotel room before lashing out, as well."

"That seems to fit your idea that the attacker was known to his or her victims," Durand said, and Gregory nodded.

"Yes, I think that's very likely."

While the police team discussed the mechanics of running a crime scene, Gregory moved slowly around the room, taking care not to tread anywhere he shouldn't and following a protective walkway the technical and scientific officers had laid out. One of them was taking photographs of Juliette—close-up, unforgiving images of a life laid bare—and he turned away to look out of the dormer window and gather his thoughts.

As he looked out of the grubby windowpanes, he understood immediately what had attracted Juliette to the apartment; from this vantage point, there was an uninterrupted view of the Eiffel Tower and the rooftops of Paris. He wondered how many times Juliette Deschamps had stood in the same spot and watched the clouds roll by—then he noticed a wooden stool that had been placed nearby with a copy of Mary Shelley's *Frankenstein* resting on top, presumably where she had often perched reading and looking out of the window.

Gregory turned to survey the rest of the room, scanning every corner, and was struck by an incredible weight of sadness. There was an emptiness here that came not only from a violent loss of life but something deeper. Even accounting for a degree of projection which came from his own grief at the senseless waste of life, it was still true that there were no pictures on the walls, nor any mementos of Juliette's travels around the world. The décor was spartan and impersonal and, if he hadn't known better, he'd have said she'd only recently moved in.

His eyes strayed back to the stiff figure on the floor, and he wondered who Juliette Deschamps had really been. The apartment didn't seem to fit with her public persona—which spoke of decadence and grooming—and he puzzled over it, until he remembered his conversation with Durand the previous day, and of a silver locket with a picture of a small girl inside.

"Have you informed her next of kin?" he asked the men gathered inside the doorway.

Three heads turned in his direction, not counting the forensics staff.

"Yes," Durand said. "I'll be paying her mother and father a visit after we finish here."

"Did Juliette have any children?"

Segal laughed at that.

"I don't see any crib, do you?"

"No," Gregory murmured, looking around the four empty walls. "I don't."

He wandered over to the sofa and imagined what the room would look like when it was transformed into a bed.

Where were the blankets? Where did she keep her special things?

He opened the doors of both wardrobes, which were fashioned out of heavy pine and laden with clothes—some of which she probably hadn't bought and had probably never worn. A woman of her status within the fashion industry was accustomed to receiving gifts from designers, in exchange for modelling their creations at events and around town.

The wardrobes were a trove of colours and textures, of shoes and bags—but there was no hidden shoebox containing her most precious possessions; those, as they would later learn, Juliette had left at her mother's home for safekeeping.

All except one.

A large wicker trunk stood in the corner of the room, and Gregory flipped open the lid with a gloved fingertip. Inside, there was a mound of pillows and a duvet, on top of which rested a soft toy in the shape of a puppy, and a silver-framed picture of Juliette smiling as she cradled a baby in her arms.

"Ah, God," he muttered, reaching for the memory Juliette had taken to bed with her each night to send her to sleep.

I smiled when you were born, too.

Gregory almost dropped the frame and spun around to look over his shoulder.

But it was only Inspector Durand.

"It gets to all of us, sometimes," he said, with a meaningful look towards the body in the centre of the room. "Twenty-three years, and I still feel it."

Gregory was about to correct him, and then snapped his mouth shut. If Durand wanted to think it was the sight of death that struck fear and loathing into his deepest soul, he'd let him.

"I found this," he said, pointing at the frame.

Durand looked at the picture and let out a soft expletive.

CHAPTER 22

Hélène Deschamps was clearing away the lunch plates when the intercom buzzed.

Anais ran to the door as she always did, expecting it to be one of her grandmother's friends who often came bearing small trinkets or sweets—or perhaps the tall, red-headed woman she called Maman.

"Attends, Anais!"

Hélène hurried to prevent the little girl from reaching up and turning the handle, but she was a moment too late and it swung open to reveal two strange men in the doorway. One was tall and smartly dressed, with dark, curling hair and green eyes. The shorter man was scruffy, smelled strongly of nicotine, and might as well have had 'POLICE' tattooed across his forehead.

Her hand reached out to draw the little girl back against her body, in a protective gesture.

"Mrs Deschamps?" Durand asked.

"Yes," she said, beginning to feel light-headed. "Is it Arthur? Has something happened? Please, tell me."

Durand pulled out his identification and gave her time to check it.

"It isn't your husband, Madame. Do you mind if we come inside? These things are best spoken of in private."

Hélène pinned a smile on her face and turned to her granddaughter.

"Anais? Why don't you go and play in your room, *petite*?"

She waited until the little girl trotted out of earshot, then led them into the sitting room, where she sat down and gripped the edge of the sofa.

"Please. Just get it over with."

"We're very sorry to tell you that your daughter, Juliette, was found murdered this morning," Durand said quietly. "Our deepest condolences to you and your family."

The words were spoken with such breath-taking simplicity that, at first, Hélène was unable to comprehend what he had told her.

She began shaking her head from side to side.

"Juliette? No. No, she's at work today, for Maison Leroux. There must be some mistake."

"I'm sorry, there's no mistake," the inspector said, as gently as he could. He'd been called upon to perform this painful duty many times before and there was no 'good' or 'right' way to convey the very worst news a parent could ever receive. It was best to do it as quickly and cleanly as possible.

"Can we call your husband, or perhaps another family member, Madame?"

She shook her head dumbly.

"Arthur—he won't—he won't be able to manage…" Her voice faltered, and she let out a gut-wrenching sob as reality crashed through her defences like a wrecking ball. "I need—I need my sister to come."

Durand put an urgent call through to Juliette's aunt, who happened to live nearby and was prepared to defer her own grief to come to the aid of her family.

"How did it happen?" Hélène spoke in an odd, distant voice, as tears fell silently down her face.

"It's still very early in the investigation," Durand told her. "We're gathering evidence at the moment."

"She—Juliette often has strange people writing to her agent," Hélène whispered. "She says it's a hazard of the job, to have people become infatuated and send her love letters. I told her—I *told* her it was dangerous."

"We'll be looking into every possible angle," Durand assured her. "And we'll be speaking to her agent too. In the meantime, if you feel able, can you tell us when you last saw Juliette?"

Hélène closed her eyes, battling the tears that continued to fall like rain.

"Yesterday," she managed. "She came for lunch and to see Anais, then left in the early evening."

"At what time?"

She gave a small shake of her head, as if to clear it.

"Seven-thirty or thereabouts."

"How did she seem to you?" Gregory asked, watching closely for any signs of shock. It was important to elicit facts, but not at the expense of her wellbeing.

Hélène thought back to the previous day, and of the ugly row they'd had in the kitchen.

You're no mother, Juliette...

It would be better if you left...

The memory of what she'd said was enough to elicit a guttural cry of pain, the sound of an animal in deepest torment, and both men surged forward to help as Hélène slumped forward and almost fell to the floor.

"I didn't mean it," she whispered. "Good God, I didn't mean what I said."

"What, Madame? What was said?"

But Hélène only shook her head, thinking of all the times she'd cut her daughter out; all the times she could have encouraged Anais to be more affectionate towards her. She raised tear-drenched eyes to look around the room at the fussy curtains and ornaments she polished religiously each week, but there wasn't one picture of her daughter so that Anais would be reminded of who had birthed her and loved her every day since. Not one image of her beautiful girl.

Hélène staggered off the sofa and rushed towards a dresser in the corner of the room.

"Madame Deschamps! Please, sit down, you don't look well—"

She was almost hysterical now, dragging open drawers so their contents fell onto the floor, and Gregory looked to Durand for his approval before rising to help.

"Madame," he said, in the same neutral, unthreatening

tone he used with all his patients. "What are you looking for?"

"Juliette," she muttered. "Her pictures. I know...I know they're here somewhere. I put them in an album to show Anais, one day. I must find them."

"You could find them later, surely?"

"No!" she shouted, and then held a hand to her lips. "I must find them now. There should be pictures of her, so Anais can see, and be proud."

As proud as she was.

"You can tell Anais all about Juliette—and share your happy memories."

Hélène nodded mutely, and although she still searched the cupboard, her hands were less frantic than before.

"Can you tell me a happy memory you have of Juliette?" Gregory asked.

She closed her eyes and an image of Juliette popped into her mind, when she'd been around eight or nine years old. Arthur hadn't been too bad, and so the three of them had boarded the train to Versailles and spent a summer's day wandering the grounds and boating on the lake. She remembered her daughter laughing as she splashed in the water fountains—innocent and free, and giggling as she dabbed ice cream on her father's nose.

So long ago.

"Her laughter," Hélène whispered, staring off into the distance.

They all turned to hear the soft pitter-patter of small feet approaching down the hall.

"Grand-mère?"

With a monumental effort, Hélène drew herself up, using the tissue Gregory offered to dry the worst of the tears from her face before facing the child. With a shaking hand, she reached for a large scrapbook at the bottom of a pile of old newspapers, and held it carefully in her arms, as if it would break.

"*Viens-ici, Anais,*" she beckoned the little girl forward when she appeared in the doorway. "Come and see your Maman. Come—come and sit with me, and see how lovely she was."

Both men knew there would be very little else Hélène Deschamps could tell them about Juliette, not as grief and shock began to take hold, but Durand ventured to ask one more question.

"Who is Anais's father, Hélène?"

The woman looked up from the scrapbook, then at the little girl who was happily turning the pages and pointing at her Maman, asking when she would be seeing her again.

"I don't know," she said honestly. "Juliette never told me, and she didn't list a name on the birth certificate either. We used to argue about it, but now I'm glad. I wouldn't want anybody to come and take Anais away from us."

Gregory watched the rosy-cheeked toddler and thought of how hard it must have been for Juliette to leave her.

"Why didn't Juliette keep Anais with her?"

Hélène sighed deeply.

"She couldn't. When Anais was born, we had very little. We lived in a bad part of the city, with barely enough to pay the bills, let alone feed another mouth. When Juliette told us the news, I was angry," she admitted. "I felt she'd wasted her life, and would regret it. God forgive me, I encouraged her to go to the clinic…but she ignored me, and I've never been so relieved."

She looked down at the girl resting in the crook of her arm and smoothed a hand over the top of her silky head.

"We were prepared to struggle, but then Juliette came home one day with an offer from Gabrielle Leroux which changed everything. They wanted to make her a model, and the money…it was too much to ignore. Juliette took it, and so did we."

So did I, she amended silently. *And punished Juliette for every cent I took, for every time my pride was hurt.*

She looked down at the scrapbook lying open on her lap and wept.

Gregory and Durand said little as they descended the lift from the Deschamps' apartment, and even less as they walked out into the mid-afternoon sunshine that bathed Paris in a golden light, which seemed so incongruous given their present sadness.

"The world continues to turn," Durand said, as they clambered inside his trusty Citröen. "We should not punish ourselves for continuing to breathe."

Through the windscreen, Gregory saw a large billboard

advertising a luxury brand of underwear. A famous French footballer posed beside a lithe, half-naked woman who looked up at him with slumberous eyes.

The woman was Juliette Deschamps.

"Yes," he said wearily. "Life goes on, Mathis. But a little girl lost her mother today."

Durand started the engine and pulled out into the main road, narrowly avoiding a collision with an oncoming car. Horns blared, and the air turned blue with phrases Alex had never heard before.

"Are you trying to kill us both?" he asked.

Durand gave one of his enigmatic smiles.

"Not yet, *mon ami*."

The traffic was light as they made their way back to the 7th Arrondissement, where Gregory was due to see Camille for their next session while Durand went back to the business of investigating Juliette's murder. But first, they had to make a pit-stop to see Leon, whose exploits in the matter of Camille's forged identity papers had not been forgotten—though the events of the morning had delayed his appointment with the Brigade Criminelle.

As they crossed the river and pootled along the Quai Voltaire which ran parallel to the water, Durand began to roll a cigarette—handily using his forearms to steer the wheel as he performed a task that clearly could not wait—and shaved another few years off Gregory's life in stress alone.

"What do you make of all this?" Durand asked, once he'd lit the rollie and cracked the window open. "Do you think we're looking for the same person in both cases?"

Gregory shaded his eyes against the dappled light which filtered through the trees lining the road and tried to visualise the sort of person capable of inflicting the brutality they'd seen that day.

"Both victims are—or were—successful models," he said. "That much is obvious and, on the face of it, we could be looking for a sexually-motivated killer. However, there was no evidence of sexual assault in Camille's case, and no obvious sign of it in Juliette's case, though we won't know for sure until the pathologist's report comes through."

"We haven't found any evidence of harassment—or at least nothing out of the ordinary," Durand said, tapping the ash from his cigarette out of the window. "Although it's still early days in the case of Juliette—and, as for Camille, we're still waiting to hear from the digital forensics team to see if anything can be traced from the memory card of her phone. Only then will we know whether there was anything incriminating."

Gregory nodded, and wondered what constituted 'ordinary' harassment.

"I'm cautious about speculating at this point, but I can make some general remarks from what we've seen," he said. "If we assume the perpetrator is the same person in both cases, we also have to assume they'd be as careful not to leave trace DNA at Juliette's apartment, as they were when they visited Camille."

Durand made a murmuring sound of agreement.

"To protect themselves in such a way would take planning. They'd need to bring a bag of some kind, containing overalls, gloves…that sort of thing."

Gregory nodded.

"Which brings me to the point: there's a contradiction between the careful, organised planning it would have taken to protect themselves from detection, and the frenzied, disorganised way this person attacked both women. The nature of the injuries was similar in both cases, but the execution was much bolder, and much less cautious with Juliette than with Camille."

Durand glanced across at Gregory.

"You think the man—the *person* we're looking for, is losing control?"

"I think there was a clear escalation in violence with Juliette," Gregory replied. "If it's the same person in both cases, then, yes, I think they're getting a taste for violence and it's making them greedy."

Durand swung his car onto the Boulevard Saint-Michel and found a parking spot near the Jardin du Luxembourg, another leafy park that had belonged to a palace of the same name before being made public.

"Leon has his studio near here," the inspector said. "But we have to walk the rest of the way because the road is closed. There's a march taking place this afternoon."

Gregory raised an eyebrow, thinking of the recent 'yellow vest' movement that had turned Paris into an urban battlefield. Civil unrest still bubbled beneath the surface of that fine city, the like of which hadn't been seen for decades.

"What's the cause?" he asked.

"Women's rights," Durand replied, and slammed the car door shut.

CHAPTER 23

The studio where Leon photographed some of the world's most beautiful people was one of those shabby-chic affairs Gregory had seen on the cover of *Interior Design Monthly*, or some equally tedious publication he'd thumbed through while waiting to be called into a dental appointment. The building was classical, like much of Paris, but the interior consisted of a duplex penthouse with acres of glass and steel, and was styled to within an inch of its life to mimic the kind of minimalist, renovated warehouse apartment Gregory happened to own on the banks of the Thames, back in London.

His furnishings, though, had been sourced from a popular brand of wallet-friendly Scandinavian homewares—and the lack of adornment came from a disinclination towards clutter rather than an eye for *feng shui*.

They were admitted by a tall, slender man who introduced himself as Raoul, and who disappeared into the kitchen after threatening to bring them both a cup of kombucha.

"Changed your mind about that photoshoot, Doctor?"

The disembodied voice came from somewhere above them, where Leon leaned against a galleried landing rail and gave them both a lazy smile.

"I see you've brought company with you, so perhaps not," he added. "I thought our appointment had been cancelled, Inspector."

Durand craned his neck to look at him, all traces of humour gone.

"Juliette Deschamps was found murdered this morning, as I'm sure you've already heard, since it was one of your assistants who discovered her body," he said. "This is no time for levity, monsieur."

Leon took his time coming down a suspended spiral glass staircase, his bare feet making little sound as he crossed the hardwood floor to greet them both properly.

"I apologise, Inspector," he said, with every appearance of sincerity. "It came as a shock to all of us, but we each have our own ways of dealing with these things. Isn't that so, Doctor?"

Gregory ignored that.

"Is this a convenient time?" he said.

Leon shrugged, which caused the chains around his neck to clink together in a clash of precious metal.

"My day is already ruined," he said, before strutting off in the direction of a large curved seating area at the other end of the cavernous space. "Make yourselves at home."

Durand smiled grimly.

"I think this one is going to be interesting," he muttered.

Gregory caught the light of battle in the inspector's eyes

and would have felt sorry for the man who called himself Leon, had he not remembered the plight of a young woman with a ruined face, and another who lay on a cold slab at the city mortuary.

"I think you may be right," he said, and gestured for him to go ahead.

The first inclination that their cosy fireside chat would not be as cosy as he had first imagined struck Leon shortly after Inspector Durand began reading him his rights.

"What is this? I thought you needed to ask some simple follow-up questions?"

Durand gave him a bland smile.

"I'm afraid some new evidence has come to light, Monsieur Boucher. Would you like to instruct a lawyer to be present while we ask you these questions? Of course, if that were the case, we would need to take you down to the police station so that all the proper procedures are observed… there is a lot of press on the streets today, ahead of the march this afternoon. I imagine they would be quite interested to hear the scoop about a second young woman having been attacked in such a short space of time, particularly as they have both been photographed by you."

"What? I've photographed *countless* women—"

"Naturally, we will do whatever you prefer."

Leon gave the little police inspector a fulminating glare and flipped his fringe off his forehead.

"I don't need a lawyer," he said.

"*D'accord*," Durand replied, and took his time drawing out a notepad and pencil while the photographer grew hot under his fashionably low collar.

Raoul bustled over with a silver tray piled high with cups of kombucha and flapjacks made entirely of healthy ingredients—thereby robbing them of their essential *raison d'être*, as far as Gregory was concerned—but promptly bustled off again looking tearful after a few unkind words from the subject of their present inquiry.

"He's beginning to bore me," Leon said, leaning back against the plump cushions with an air of supreme arrogance.

Gregory watched him with interest, studying his gestures and mannerisms as if he were a specimen, taking mental notes for future cases. Sufferers of narcissistic personality disorder always made fascinating subjects, and Leon had certainly displayed several of the key attributes associated with that condition: an exaggerated sense of self-importance; a clear sense of entitlement, requiring excessive admiration from others; and a preoccupation with fantasies about brilliance or power—not to mention a total inability to recognise the feelings of others.

"Let's make this quick," Leon said sharply. "There are more important things I could be doing."

"More important than assisting a murder investigation?" Gregory said mildly.

Leon folded his arms across his chest.

"Why are you here, anyway? You're not with the police."

"No, but he's our consultant, and the Commissaire herself has given permission for Doctor Gregory to attend," Durand said. "Now, let's turn to the matters in hand."

He glanced down at his notebook, purely for show, then fixed Leon Boucher with one of his best smiles.

"When was the first time you met Wendy Li?"

The blood drained from the other man's face, but he rallied as quickly as he could.

"I—I don't know anybody called Wendy Li."

Durand heaved a sigh.

"Leon, we've already spoken to Wendy. She told us everything."

Gregory glanced at the inspector from the corner of his eye but said nothing.

"That's impossible," Leon said, swallowing hard.

"How so? Madame Li was perfectly happy to talk—"

Leon laughed at that.

"Wendy would never talk to the po—"

He snapped his mouth shut, but not before the damage had been done.

"It always surprises me how well that little trick works," Durand said, conversationally. "Now that we understand one another, Leon, let's not beat around the bush anymore. You are the one who referred Camille Duquette to Wendy Li, where she was able to procure certain forged identity documents. Is that correct?"

"I—I think I want a lawyer," Leon said, swallowing hard as he looked around the designer duplex and imagined it all crashing around his ears.

"That's your right," Durand said, amiably. "Unfortunately, I will need to refer the matter to my superiors—who are likely to recommend that you're arrested and brought in for formal questioning at the station. I'll just make that call, while you instruct your lawyer—"

Leon swore viciously, then held up a hand.

"Wait—alright, look," he said, sounding considerably less confident than before. "It isn't what you might think."

"And what am I thinking, Leon?" Durand enquired, in a deceptively placid tone. "Shall I tell you? I think you knowingly lied to the police, on more than one occasion, when asked directly whether you knew any other pertinent facts relating to Camille Duquette's attack—and lied *again* when you said you knew nothing about her identity. Do you know what the penalty is for deceiving a police officer in the course of his duties?"

Leon was sweating hard.

"I didn't lie when I said I know nothing about her identity—I still don't…"

Durand laughed.

"Come on, Leon. You don't expect us to believe that?"

"It's true!" he insisted. "When she came to me for the test shoot, after Gabrielle discovered her, she introduced herself as Camille Duquette. I never thought anything of it…but, later…she told me she needed to leave. I said the shoot wasn't over, but she was adamant."

He relaxed a bit, getting into the swing of his story, and Gregory silently ticked '*enjoys having the attention of an audience*' off the list.

"Naturally, I told her that, if she left then, she could consider her career over before it had even begun. She didn't like that," he said, lifting a cup of kombucha to his lips. "She said she probably couldn't take the job, anyway, and I asked her why. She said she didn't have the right paperwork, or even a bank account, so there was no point in continuing."

He set the cup back on the tray with a shaky hand, and then clasped his fingers together.

"I know what that feels like," he admitted. "To fall between the cracks, to have nothing to my name. Years ago, I was refused refugee status despite living through hell, seeing horrors you could not imagine. I dreamed of a beautiful world, so I made my own way out and came to the world's most beautiful city."

Gregory's eyes strayed to the fire-damaged skin on the man's neck and wondered again how he had come by it.

"The people who helped me through Germany, they told me about a woman called Wendy Li. They said she was the best, but she charged top dollar. I had nothing—no money, no connections…but I could draw a scene with my eyes closed. I went to her and offered to work in exchange for new papers. I ended up staying for two years."

"And you recommended her to Camille?"

Leon nodded.

"She seemed so desperate. I recognised something in her," he said, rubbing his hands back and forth in a nervous motion. "I felt sorry for her, I suppose."

No, Gregory thought. *You don't feel sorry for anyone.*

It was far more likely he'd come to some kind of financial arrangement with Camille, in exchange for the introduction.

"Did she tell you anything about her previous identity?" he asked.

"No more lies, Leon," Durand warned. "You're in it up to your neck, as it is."

At the mention of it, the photographer rubbed a hand over the mottled skin at his neck, and nodded.

"It's no lie," he repeated. "She never told me her real name, and I never asked. I assumed she wanted to forget her 'old' self, just as I wanted to forget mine."

"And who was he?" Gregory murmured.

Leon thought of the skinny, bow-legged boy he'd once been, and shook his head.

"He's dead."

CHAPTER 24

Gregory left Inspector Durand to continue his interrogation of Leon Boucher, while he returned to see Camille Duquette. According to her nurse, she'd spent a peaceful night sleeping for eight solid hours and had woken happily enough, spending most of the morning sitting by the window or reading her book. However, her day nurse called to report a worrying dip in Camille's mood, and asked him to attend immediately.

On the journey across town, Gregory catalogued the drugs she was taking, none of which were anti-psychotics or anti-depressants he might have associated with unexplained mood swings. In the absence of any obvious medicinal side-effects, he stepped through all the known symptoms of dissociative amnesia and came to the obvious conclusion.

Camille was experiencing a breakthrough.

He paid off the taxi driver—whose driving had been sedate in comparison with what he'd grown accustomed to, lately—and hurried upstairs to help however he could.

Agnés, the day nurse, was waiting for him at the door.

"Thank God," she muttered. "She's through there, in the living room. I must tell you, I was forced to restrain her at one point, for her own safety."

"Why?"

"It was the same as before," she said, clearly distressed by the experience. "One moment, she was completely docile, sitting having a sandwich. The next moment—*mon Dieu*—she threw the plate across the room and demanded to know why she was being held captive."

She wrung her hands.

"*Captive*? I told her, it is not like that at all. I explained she cannot remember simple things and had been badly injured, so it was best I stayed with her, so she did not hurt herself. As God is my witness, monsieur, I told her, I would take her out for a walk to the park, or to the shop…"

"All right Agnés, it's all right," he murmured, shrugging out of his jacket. "Has she asked to see anyone?"

"She asked to see Madeleine or Juliette."

Gregory's head whipped around, both surprised and elated.

She remembered.

"Have you given her any sedative?" he asked, and the nurse shook her head.

"You said to avoid it, so I held her firmly in my arms until she quietened down. She wasn't happy about it, but she seems to be a little more stable than before. She's still asking to see a mirror."

Gregory mulled it over, but shook his head.

"I need to do an updated risk assessment, considering this afternoon's incident," he said. "I'll make a decision on that after I've spoken to her."

"I can hear you whispering about me!" a voice suddenly bellowed, so loudly they were both startled. "Who's that? Is it Gabrielle or Armand?"

Gregory hardly recognised the tone to Camille's voice; it was so different from the softly spoken woman he'd met the day before. As he entered the living room, he realised that wasn't the only thing that had changed.

"Who're you?"

Camille was standing beside the window, her long legs encased in a pair of skin-tight leggings and a baggy tee-shirt she'd knotted at the waist. Her scar was hidden from view behind the long fall of her dark hair, and everything about her stance spoke of a woman who knew she was beautiful—scars, or no scars.

"Did you hear what I said?"

Gregory walked into the room slowly, tucking his hands into the pockets of his trousers, and Camille gave him a very thorough, very feminine assessment, which had been noticeably absent the day before.

"Don't you remember me?" he asked, coming to stand a careful distance away. "We met yesterday, and the day before that."

Bold blue eyes scanned his face and body, then she gave a decisive shake of her head.

"Do you work for Leroux?" she asked.

Gregory didn't know what to make of this turn of events. The day before, Camille had been unable to recall long-term memories but, now, the situation seemed to have reversed.

It was highly irregular.

"My name is Doctor Alexander Gregory," he said, and waited for any reaction—but there was none. "Do you know why you're here?"

"That person—the nurse—told me I'd been attacked," Camille said, jerking her chin towards Agnés, who practically cowered behind him. "Obviously, I can feel the bandages, but she won't let me see for myself, in a mirror. I don't know what the hell's going on."

Gregory was beginning to see the 'Camille' that Leon had spoken of.

"Do you mind if I sit down?" he asked, feeling an uncomfortable sense of déja-vu.

"Do as you please," she muttered, still watching him with her assessing blue gaze. "Are you English?"

He nodded.

"It seems I wear my nationality on my sleeve," he said, with a smile.

Her lips twitched.

"You're not so bad," she said, generously. "Out of practice, maybe."

He acknowledged the truth of that.

"I'm here because the Brigade Criminelle asked me to help them investigate your attack."

"Why? Don't they know how to do their jobs?"

He almost laughed, and silently added 'candid' to her list of personality traits.

"They know very well," he replied. "But, without a suspect, or any witnesses, they were struggling to understand the kind of person who would attack you in such a way."

"And where do you come in?"

He'd asked himself the same thing many times before, but Gregory took the question at face value.

"I'm a psychologist and a criminal profiler," he said, letting the admission roll around on his tongue. Until a few weeks ago, he would have gone to great pains to avoid the label, but it seemed most apt for the job he appeared to be doing.

"What does that mean? You rub a crystal ball?"

He smiled again, and this time she smiled back.

"If only it were that easy," he said, with feeling. "I help police forces to narrow their pool of available suspects, usually in cases where there's very little evidence to go on."

"What do you mean, 'little evidence'?" she demanded, and raised a hand to touch the bandage on her face. "Wouldn't you say this was ample proof?"

Her eyes suddenly swam with tears.

"I don't need to see it to know how bad it is," she said, quietly. "It hurts to speak, and the fact nobody will let me see it…it must be very bad. My career is finished. I know that much."

A single tear spilled over.

"I'm sorry for what's happened to you, Camille," he said. "But nothing is ever as bad as it seems. You've been suffering severe trauma and memory loss, which has made you vulnerable. For that reason, it isn't a good idea for you to see the physical injuries until we can be sure your mind will process the visual information it receives in a reasonable way. If you panic, you may do something silly."

She pulled a face.

"Like what? Kill myself?"

Gregory said nothing; he would never make light of suicide, having seen the after-effects at Southmoor and spending most of his time trying hard to prevent it.

But you were too late for me, weren't you?

His mother's voice whispered in his ear and Gregory stiffened, fighting the urge to look around. It was nothing more than a phantom memory; a projection of his deepest guilt.

There was no such thing as ghosts.

"Do you—ah, can you tell me what you remember of the attack?" he asked, once the black spots behind his eyes had faded.

She shook her head.

"I don't remember," she said, raising a hand to massage her head. "It—I get a headache, when I try to think about it."

"All right," he said gently. "Let's try something else. Tell me the first thing that pops into your mind."

"Monet's Garden, at Giverny," she said promptly.

"Is Giverny special to you, Camille? That's the second time you've mentioned it."

"Is it?"

She gave a frustrated sigh and moved to sit in the chair opposite, in exactly the same spot she'd occupied the previous day, except, this time, she tucked her feet up and slouched against the arm, resting her head on her hand.

"I really don't know," she said. "You just said to tell you the first thing that sprang to mind. I thought of Giverny."

Gregory nodded.

"What else can you remember?" he asked. "Can you tell me where you were born?"

She opened her mouth to answer what should have been an easy question.

"I—I can't remember," she said, with rising panic. "It's on the tip of my tongue—"

"How about telling me how old you are, instead?"

"Um, twenty-four," she replied. "But please don't tell Leroux. I told them I was nineteen."

She gave a self-conscious shrug.

She looked it, Gregory thought. With her face bare of make-up, wearing gym gear, she looked five years younger than she was, and youth was a valuable asset in the fashion industry.

"You couldn't seem to remember your age, yesterday," he remarked.

"I couldn't? Why not?"

He smiled, wondering how long they had to talk about neural connectors in the brain.

"Your mind is traumatised," he said. "It's processing information and feeding old memories back to you in a haphazard way. Yesterday, you remembered me, whereas today, you don't."

She smiled suddenly, in a very feline way.

"I'm sure I would remember you."

Gregory ignored that and moved on to the next question.

"What about Leon?" he asked. "Do you remember anybody by that name?"

"Of course," she laughed. "Everybody in the fashion world knows Leon. He's the best photographer in the industry."

Of course he is, Gregory thought. *Especially by his own estimation.*

"And does the name Wendy Li mean anything to you?"

A cloud passed over her face, and she was quiet for a long moment.

"I think I know the name," she said. "But I can't remember how."

He remained silent. Sometimes, it was the most effective tool.

"I can remember what she looks like," Camille continued, after a couple of seconds. "She's an old Chinese woman. Very small, with very thin hands. I think…it sounds stupid, but I think she does palm readings."

She looked at him in confusion.

"Why would I go to have a palm reading?" she said. "It's nonsense."

Gregory thought about how accurate his own had been, but said nothing of that.

"You don't remember anything else about her?" he asked.

"Do you remember meeting her?"

She held her head in her hand and visibly struggled, before her shoulders slumped.

"It's like—it's like trying to grasp onto a puff of smoke," she muttered. "Like waking up after a dream. You think it'll stay vivid and real, but it floats away."

"It may come back to you," he said, and suddenly the procureur's voice echoed around his mind.

She's having you on, mon ami.

"You seem to remember the Leroux very well," he said, thrusting aside the self-doubt that nipped at the edges of his mind. "Can you tell me more about them?"

"Maison Leroux is one of the best fashion houses in the world. Gabrielle asked me to model for them at Fashion Week."

She proclaimed it proudly, then her smile faded as she remembered the reason why she was there. "I've missed my chance, now," she whispered.

"Do you remember when you first met Gabrielle?"

Yesterday, it had been a difficult question but, today, it seemed an easy one.

"Sure, it was a few weeks ago," she said, without hesitation. "I ran into her on the street, on the Place Vendome."

"What were you doing there?" he asked.

Once again, she opened her mouth, but no sound came out.

"I—I must have been—I'm not sure. It was at night."

He nodded, making a note.

"All right. What did Gabrielle say?"

"She said I had a great 'look'," Camille replied, dully. "She asked me if I'd ever considered modelling."

"Had you?"

"What?"

"Wanted to be a model, as a little girl?"

"I—I don't know. I can't remember anything before meeting Gabrielle."

Gregory steepled his forefinger and thumb against his temple, considering the best way to approach the problem.

"What about Armand? Do you remember the first time you met him?"

"Sure," she said. "It was at a party he and his wife threw to welcome their new 'family'. They call us 'family' so that we'll all try and get along."

"And, do you? Get along?"

She nodded.

"Well enough," she said. "Some people never like fresh blood on the scene, so they make things difficult. I don't mind that."

There was the hard-nosed side again, he thought.

"You were telling me about Armand."

"Oh, yeah. There isn't much to tell, really. He leaves his wife to make the creative decisions while he eats, or makes phone calls, or sleeps on a sofa somewhere."

That sounded about right, Gregory had to admit.

"Camille, do you know anybody who would wish to hurt you? Do you remember anything at all about your attack?"

She ran a nervous hand through her hair, then touched gentle fingers to the bandage on her cheek.

"I—all I remember is the pain," she said, choking back fresh tears. "And anger. They seemed so *angry.*"

He leaned forward.

"They? Camille, do you think it was a man or a woman who attacked you? Try to visualise their face—"

But she started to cry softly, wrapping her arms around her body as she rocked back and forth.

"I—I can't," she whispered. "I can't."

———

Gregory tried to work around her mental blocks for a while longer, reversing this way and that, but, by the end of their conversation, Camille was exhausted. He elicited a promise that she should call him or the nurse if she felt frightened or panicked, and promised in return to take her for a walk the following day, once she'd regained her strength.

Her eyes barely staying open, Camille agreed, and Agnés reappeared to draw the curtains and tuck her into bed for a nap.

"If she has another episode, call me straight away," Gregory murmured, once she had fallen into a dead sleep. "Her mind is extremely fragile and, to tell you the truth, I don't know which version of Camille you'll get the next time she wakes up."

The nurse nodded, looking across at the woman the press still called 'Sleeping Beauty'.

"Do you think she'll recover?"

"She's already recovering," he replied. "Her memories are coming back thick and fast but, unfortunately, not fast enough. If she could only remember something of the attack, it might be the key to everything."

As he was preparing to leave, there came a knock at the door.

He waved Agnés away and checked the peephole, surprised to find that particular visitor standing in the hallway outside.

"Madeleine?"

He opened the door and drank in the sight of her.

"I'm sorry to disturb you," she said shyly. "I spoke to Procureur Segal, and he said it was alright to visit—"

Gregory held off making any inflammatory remarks about the prosecutor's ability to judge a patient's fitness to receive visitors, since it was a moot point.

"Camille's asleep at the moment," he told her. "And I'm afraid she's had a rough day."

"Oh—I'm sorry to hear that," she said, looking down at the small bunch of flowers she'd brought with her. "Would it be alright to leave these for her?"

He smiled, wondering what it was about her that he found so appealing. She had beauty, yes; but there were many kinds of beauty, and the most obvious seldom appealed to him. There had to be something else, something more substantial than the shape of her face and the lines of her body—though, as a red-blooded heterosexual male, he wasn't hypocrite enough to deny their appeal.

"I'm singing at the Café Laurent again tonight," Madeleine was saying. "I was planning to have an early dinner, if you'd like to join me?"

The nurse made a good show of pretending not to listen, as she took the flowers to douse them in water.

"Ah—"

He hesitated, grappling between Doctor Gregory and Alex, uncertain as to who presently had the upper hand.

"If you're busy, it's no problem," she said, huskily. "I heard what happened to Juliette, so you must be busy helping the police with their investigation."

And he heard the grief that was written all over her face, as well as the fear.

He had a report to write and some research to do but, after that...

"See you at five?"

She smiled brilliantly and reached up to bestow a soft kiss, before heading back out into the sunny Autumn afternoon.

Before he could make his own way out, Agnés's voice stopped him.

"Careful, Doctor. You wouldn't be the first to be blinded by a pretty face."

Wise words, he thought, and worth remembering.

CHAPTER 25

"We lost another one, Bill."

Gregory watched a group of tourists passing by, from his position at the window seat of a café at the summit of the Trocadéro, a hill overlooking the Eiffel Tower from the north side of the River Seine, not far from the Arc de Triomphe. It was the perfect spot to take pictures, and people swarmed the wide palazzo-style terrace to capture the perfect image to put on their mantelpiece, while his thoughts turned to murder.

"Tell me about it," his friend invited.

It was mid-morning in Boston, and Professor Bill Douglas had another speech to prepare, but it could wait.

"Juliette Deschamps, model and mother of one," Gregory said simply. "Young, with everything to live for."

Douglas heard the sadness in his friend's voice and was sorry for it. Their work left bruises on the heart, ones that never fully healed.

"I seem to recognise the name," he said.

"You may well do," Gregory said, as a television fixed to the far wall of the café began to roll out the early evening news and a picture of Juliette filled the entire screen beside the words 'BUTCHER STRIKES AGAIN'. "She's the face of various perfume and lingerie brands, but she was also one of the women who overheard Camille Duquette's attack."

"That's interesting," Douglas said. "Do the police think that's the motive—to silence her?"

"They're not committed to any particular theory at the moment, but I think it's an interesting coincidence. Firstly, how would Camille's attacker know that Juliette was staying next door, or that she was a witness, unless they had inside knowledge or sight of the police file?"

Gregory watched the news reporter speak in serious, urgent tones outside Juliette's apartment, where the Technical and Scientific Officers were still working. By now, a forensics tent had been erected outside the main entrance and the other occupants of the building evacuated to nearby hotels to allow the investigative work to continue, but it made for sombre viewing.

Unbidden, an image of Juliette's body floated into his mind and he swore softly, raising an espresso cup to his lips to drain the last of the strong hot liquid in an effort to cleanse himself.

"What's that?" Douglas said.

"Nothing, sorry, I was distracted for a moment. The other thing to consider is what possible reason Camille's attacker could have for wanting to silence Juliette; the police already know they're at large."

"Unless she knew more than she let on," Douglas said. "Perhaps the girl saw who it was, and threatened to blackmail them."

"Surely that would come out in her phone messages or calls?"

"Not if they spoke directly," Douglas argued. "As you said yourself, it could be someone already known to both women. Which means—"

"It could be someone in their everyday circle," Gregory finished. "Yes, that makes sense. Juliette could talk easily with someone she was already due to see."

"How is Camille's recovery coming along?" Douglas enquired. "She's still an important missing piece in this puzzle—if she could only remember some details."

"I was thinking the very same thing," Gregory said. "She's still displaying the classic symptoms of dissociative amnesia, by repressing traumatic memories and converting them into physical symptoms, predominantly headaches and migraines."

Douglas leaned back in his chair, while his encyclopaedic mind rolled back over his long career to find other examples of a case like hers.

"She's been recovering from injuries," he remarked. "We can't say for certain that her migraines are wholly psychosomatic; they may be a genuine physical response."

Gregory raised a hand to order another coffee.

"I would agree, but they tend to come on during our discussions, particularly when I'm pressing her to try to recall basic information about her life."

"Which she doesn't want to do?"

"Not at all," Gregory said. "On the policing side, we found out Camille sourced fresh identity paperwork, but we're still no closer to uncovering her real name. It's interesting that, when I visited her today, she hardly blinked when I referred to her as Camille, whereas yesterday it would have distressed her."

"Different memories coming to the fore," Douglas muttered. "The fabric of our memories and experience make up the people we are. If Camille remembered only the last couple of weeks during which she lived a glamorous life, it's natural she would associate with that side to her personality. Yesterday, when she couldn't recall anything of her life as a model, she disassociated from it because she had no frame of reference."

Gregory agreed.

"It's unusual, don't you think? Memories that are regained don't usually slip away again, the following day."

"Dissociative amnesia can create temporary shifts in personality," he said. "A shy person becomes more outgoing, and vice versa, when they have a limited frame of reference."

Gregory looked out of the window, but he didn't see the crowds or the streets of Paris.

"I know we don't use the term 'hysteria' any longer, but I still think of it when I'm talking about dissociative illnesses like the amnesia Camille is experiencing, or cases of extreme somatization disorder," he said, referring to those patients who converted their negative experiences into extreme physical ailments, without any real pathological cause. "It struck me as odd, thinking about the origin of the word."

"It comes from the Greek *utera,* meaning 'uterus'," Douglas said. "It's a very self-limiting phrase, if it fails to allow for the possibility of similar symptoms in men."

"Exactly," Gregory murmured. "In the early days, people thought women who displayed symptoms of 'hysteria' were possessed by evil spirits—they'd have called an exorcist, not a psychologist. There's a women's rights march in Paris today, and I couldn't help wondering whether there's something else underlying all this. Something insidious that has less to do with those two women, than with the world they lived in."

Gregory watched a motorcade of police squad cars speed past the café, sirens blazing, and knew they had been called in to quell the protests.

"You're thinking they got caught up in something, and their femininity was used against them? Harassment of some kind, perhaps?"

Gregory thought of Armand Leroux and his reputation with women, and wondered.

"Something's rumbling beneath all this, but I can't put my finger on it."

"It could be much simpler than you think," Douglas said, playing devil's advocate. "The danger in our business is over-thinking matters, and looking for complicated explanations when the simplest may be the most appropriate. It could be your run-of-the-mill serial killer on the loose, and he has a refined taste for pretty young women."

"Since when did serial killers become 'run-of-the-mill'?" Gregory said, with a smile.

"You know what I mean. If we stripped away all the unique circumstances of Camille's identity fraud and her peculiar psychological response to trauma, we'd be left with—sadly—another young woman fallen prey to attack, most likely from someone who developed an unhealthy fixation and wildly inappropriate fantasies about violence. They're easier to profile, for one thing."

"Easier to profile, maybe—but harder to find."

Douglas blew out a breath.

"You don't have to find the bastard, you only have to build up a picture of what their mind looks like. Leave the police to do their job, Alex, while you concentrate on yours. There may be something you've missed."

Long after the call ended, Gregory remained seated to watch the news report that was still rolling on the television across the room. The faces of two women now filled the screen, the press having assumed a connection between the victims based on their profession alone.

Perhaps Douglas was right.

Maybe it was that simple.

CHAPTER 26

As Gregory made his way to meet Madeleine Paquet, two other people met at a tiny bar on the Île Saint-Louis. The area was one of two natural islands in the River Seine, accessible via four bridges, including one connecting it to the larger Île de la Cité that was home to Notre-Dame, as well as the former headquarters of the Brigade Criminelle. It was a historic part of town and, whilst the land might once have been used to graze cattle, it was now an upmarket stalwart of the 4th Arrondissement.

"It's dangerous to be seen here."

The other smiled genially.

"On the contrary, it's the safest place to be. Nobody from the PJ would come here to drink; it's far too close to the office. Besides, the place is full of tourists. Who would know or remember our faces?"

They paused as a fresh group of students piled into the drinking hole, laden with backpacks and selfie sticks, and they barely glanced at the pair seated in the corner.

"I need to ask whether you're involved."

The other took a swig of red wine, then set it carefully back on the marble-topped table.

"You need to ask?"

"*Yes.*"

"What do you think?"

"You're being evasive," the other hissed. "Just answer me. I need to know."

"Surely, it's better for someone in your position to remain in ignorance. If anything should come to light, it will look bad for both of us. At least, this way, you can deny all knowledge."

"Will anything come to light?"

"Not if we're careful."

"The profiler—"

"Hasn't got a clue," the other snapped. "Camille can't tell him anything and, as for the other one, she can't say very much now, can she?"

It was heartless but true, and there was a certain comfort to that.

"Gregory will be leaving in a few days, and then it will be back to business as usual. Drink up and forget your worries—they'll be forgotten, soon enough."

But as the outer door opened, it brought a gust of cool air and a group of all-female protesters, who were celebrating a day well spent, their animated voices already chattering about the next time they would take to the streets. They carried cardboard banners with slogans on one side and pasted photographs of Juliette and Camille on the other.

'*JE SUIS ELLE, ET ELLE EST MOI*', one slogan read.
I am she, and she is me.

And the pair in the corner knew a moment's fear, for there were some who refused to be forgotten, even in death.

Madeleine was waiting for him at a table beside the window, and this time she'd dressed in the post-war style, her blonde hair swept up in a victory roll with a slash of red lipstick and a polka-dot tea dress. She was the sort of woman who could choose to be conspicuous or not, and when he remarked on it, she gave him a self-deprecating smile.

"I read a magazine article once, about Marilyn Monroe," she said. "I don't know whether it was true, but the story goes that she was walking one day in New York City with a friend, who asked why people weren't mobbing her in the street, clamouring for her autograph. Marilyn asked her friend whether they'd like to see her 'become Marilyn' and, when she did, something subtle changed—her body language, the way she moved—and suddenly cars were slowing down and people were staring at her."

Gregory listened as he shrugged out of his overcoat and hung it on a peg on the wall.

"Is that what you do? Turn on the jazz?"

She smiled at the reference.

"I think that's what we all do—each of us who are asked to play a role. We switch between different sides of ourselves."

"What side am I seeing now?" he asked.

Madeleine smiled slowly.

"I suppose you're seeing Margot. She's fun, relaxed and generally happy."

Gregory wondered if she knew how sad that sounded.

"And Madeleine?"

"Is taking the night off," she said. "Her work is done, for a few days at least."

She broke a breadstick in half and offered a piece to him.

"Which side of you am I seeing?" she asked, throwing the question back.

"Very good," he murmured. "It's a bad habit of mine, to ask all the questions and answer none myself."

"What do they call that in your world—*avoidance*?"

They looked at each other for a long moment, enjoying the brief electricity, then he leaned back to break the contact.

"What a pity, I rather liked your alter-ego," she murmured.

"But not this one?"

He said it with a smile, but the question was serious. 'Doctor Gregory' was the man he embodied most of the time, and most in need of acceptance.

"I like him very much, too," she said. "He's a bit uptight, you know, but he appreciates jazz music, and listens when I talk. He has sad green eyes he tries to hide, and is a little lost, I think…just like me."

Embarrassed, he looked away.

"Shall we order?"

She nodded, wondering if he knew how attractive it was when the cool, steady-handed Doctor Gregory was flustered.

"The casserole is good here."

"Two casseroles it is, then," he said, not bothering to look at the menu.

She leaned forward and rested her forearms on the table between them. Her hands were open, and he could have taken them in his own.

But he didn't.

"A couple of officers from Durand's team came to see me today," she said, changing the subject. "They wanted to ask me about Juliette."

Gregory caught the quick flash of pain.

"She was your friend?"

"Yes," she said quietly. "She was prickly at first, and kept to herself most of the time, but over the past couple of years we grew to know one another. I called her my friend, and she came to some of my gigs."

She looked down at her hands, then back up again.

"It wasn't common knowledge, but Juliette had a daughter she was supporting. Anais, she was called. Juliette showed me a picture once, but she preferred not to talk about her while she was in 'work mode.'"

"Yes, I know," he said, and thought back to the painful conversation with Juliette's mother. "At least she has loving grandparents to look after her."

He left the statement hanging in the air, wondering if Madeleine would choose to share any information she might have about Anais's father, but none was forthcoming.

Madeleine took a sip of water to wet her throat, which was suddenly dry.

"Last night, I told you that you didn't really know me—"

"How could I? We've only just met," he said, reasonably.

"Yes, but…what I mean is, there's another side to me that I prefer not to think about. Just like Juliette."

Whether it was the note in her voice or the look in her eye, he didn't know, but Gregory broke his own rule and reached across the table to take her hand.

"You can tell me anything," he said, and meant it. A great part of his job was to help those in emotional need, listening to their stories without judgment. He wondered if the same applied to fledgling romantic relationships, too.

"I haven't told anyone," she said, and looked around the room to check their conversation would not be overheard. "Not even the police. If it gets out to the press, my career will be ruined."

"You can rely on my discretion but, if what you tell me could help to find Juliette's killer, and Camille's attacker, I have a duty to report it to the police."

She raised a hand to cup his cheek, taking him by surprise.

"Why do you think I'm telling you this?" she murmured. "I know you'll do the right thing, whatever that may be."

He opened his mouth to tell her about his mother, Cathy Jones, and the lengths he'd gone to, to treat her illness—and the risks he'd taken to try to exact the truth, an apology, or preferably both. All for nothing, in the end.

Had he done the *right thing* there?

"A couple of years ago, when I was just starting out in the business, I made a stupid mistake," Madeleine continued, and the moment was lost.

He gave her hands a squeeze.

"People do," he said quietly. "It's called 'being human.'"

She gave him a weak smile, and hoped he would feel the same compassion once her story was told.

"Juliette and I were at the same party one night," she began. "We were told to go, because a lot of important industry people would be there, but I remember we stuck together a lot of the time because we hardly knew anyone. The club was a big place, very dark, and I was tired of smiling at the end of a long week. We found a sitting room and there was a small crowd in there already, with some of the other models we knew, so we joined them."

Madeleine drew her hands away, clasping them on her lap.

"They offered us some pills—ecstasy, I think. They said it would give us both a boost, so we'd sparkle for the people who mattered. It was so stupid...but, I took one. So did Juliette. Shortly after, I started feeling sick. The room was spinning, and I thought I was going to pass out...then, the police came."

She closed her eyes, remembering the terrifying loss of control.

"I remember being in the police car...and then Armand being there, speaking to the man in charge. I thought I would be arrested, but instead they drove me home—Juliette, too.

When I woke up the next day, Armand came to see me again and said he'd already spoken with the police. I felt terrible, worse than I can ever remember, and I thought he'd come to tell me I was fired. I'd just been offered a campaign for Petit Leroux, their children's concession, and if it ever got out that I'd been involved in a drug raid it would ruin the wholesome image they wanted to create of a young mother and her cute, well-dressed kids."

She pulled a face at that.

"But he didn't fire you?"

Gabrielle shook her head, pausing while the waiter delivered her chicken casserole, her appetite completely gone.

"He told me I could carry on working and he'd do what he could to smooth things over with the police, if I did him a favour in return," she said, feeling sick at the very thought. "He—he said he had a friend who was having another party, and he asked me to go along and be *nice* to his guests."

Gregory felt anger course through his body, so swift and so strong, he began to shake.

"You mean, he wanted you to be an escort?"

She nodded.

"That's a polite way of putting it," she said. "But Armand, he knows how to pick them. He has friends in the police, so he probably looked into our backgrounds and found out Juliette had a baby and a family to support. She couldn't afford to lose the job she'd only just begun, and neither could I. My mother requires constant care because she has advanced multiple sclerosis. The drugs she needs are new on the market and very expensive, so I need to keep working."

"He abused his position."

"Yes," she agreed. "Armand threatened to blacken our names if we told anyone about it—and I've seen it happen, Alex. I've seen models with a shining future go from being the face of huge fashion brands, to being unemployed and unemployable, practically overnight, simply on the word of one or two powerful people."

"You're afraid he'll do the same to you?"

"Yes," she said miserably. "I would love to have the confidence to stand up and speak out, and deal with the consequences later, but I have my mother to think of. The medicine has changed her life."

"Does he still ask you to go along to parties?"

"Not for over a year," she said. "He's found some fresh blood in the meantime, and I've been trying to carve out a new career, making a name for myself in the jazz clubs so I can give it up and get away. But I have to do it slowly and carefully."

"You said the police were complicit," he prompted. "Give me a name, Madeleine."

"Alex, I wish I could—"

"You can. Please."

But she shook her head, battling tears of anger and frustration.

"I want to tell you, but I'm afraid of what will happen. You don't know what these people are like, Alex. They live on another plane, where they believe they're invincible."

Oh yes, he thought. *I know people like that.*
His father was one of them.

"Do you think Juliette's death is connected to all this?"

She shook her head.

"I don't know. It happened over two years ago, so I don't understand why anybody would want to hurt her now; surely, they'd have acted back then, not after she'd done as she was told, and remained quiet."

Maybe she had a change of heart, Gregory thought. It was possible she'd given her killer a reason to act swiftly, but the manner of her death was inconsistent with the usual cases of 'punishment' or 'execution-style' killings he'd seen before. In those cases, the killer wasted no time on ritual or bloody deaths; they moved swiftly and cleanly to silence a person who had become any kind of threat.

Unless, of course, Juliette's killer was an opportunist who tried to emulate the details of Camille's attack in order to give a false impression that the perpetrator was one and the same.

If that was the case, the job for the Brigade Criminelle became much harder because they were no longer looking for one person.

They were looking for two.

"I understand if…if you don't see me the same way, now," Madeleine said, with as much bravado as she could muster. "I'm not proud of my past."

Gregory shoved aside the questions circling his mind and focused on the person seated in front of him, giving her his full attention as so few people were able to do.

"Everybody has regrets, Madeleine," he said. "Without them, we'd be two-dimensional, cardboard cut-outs without any texture or personality. I have my own regrets, and sometimes I wish I could turn back the clock to do things differently, but I can't—and neither can you. All you can do is what you've done, which is take control of your future."

He reached across to take her hand again.

"What you've told me makes me sad and angry, and you're right that I see you differently now. Before, I thought you were lovely—but now, I think you're exceptional."

Her eyes filled.

"You really mean that?"

He raised her hand to his lips and pressed a kiss to her soft skin.

"If you find the courage to tell me more of what happened, I'll be here to listen. Until you do, we won't know who we can trust at the Police Judiciaire."

She nodded mutely.

"I don't know the name," she said. "All I know is that Armand called them *le cochon*."

The pig, Gregory thought. International derogatory slang for police, of non-specific gender.

"You never met them, at one of these parties Armand arranged?"

"I was—it…" Her voice faltered and she gulped down some more water while he waited, endlessly patient. "You don't understand. These parties were like…did you ever see the film, *Eyes Wide Shut*?"

He nodded, and felt his heart sink.

"Like that," she muttered. "Everybody wore masks, and nobody used their real name. I think my drinks may have been spiked, because the memories are unclear."

"Do you know where the parties were held?"

"Everywhere," she replied. "Large houses, mostly, or rented space around the city."

Gregory could see the physical effort it was taking for her to recount what she considered to be the most shameful part of her past, and he knew they'd reached a tipping point. Two other models had been attacked in the same week— both of whom were known to her, and one of whom had experienced the same abuse of power. The similarities may be coincidence, but a police inspector friend he'd met in the North of England had once told him that there was no such thing as 'coincidence'.

He was starting to think he may be right.

"I don't think you should be alone this evening," he said.

Madeleine shook her head and gave him a private smile.

"There is safety in numbers," she agreed.

CHAPTER 27

Sunday 29ᵗʰ September

The room was dark and sumptuous, awash with velvet and silk.

The air was heavy with the stench of spoiling fruit and, when he turned, Alex saw an enormous bowl rotting away in the centre of a long, polished table. On the wall behind it was a photograph of the fruit bowl as it had once been; ripe and colourful, spilling over with fat purple grapes and shiny red apples.

But then, the image shifted, and the colours altered until it no longer showed things as they had once been, but as they now were—stale and festering.

He turned away, stumbling through a draped curtain into the next room, where another tableau awaited him.

It was a hall of mirrors but different to the one before; warmly lit and furnished in golds and reds. Banners hung from the ceiling depicting images of women of all ages, races and sizes, bearing the slogan, '*JE SUIS ELLE, ET ELLE EST MOI*'.

In the centre of the room, two women stood half-clothed, their faces concealed behind velvet masks, each holding a cardboard sign.

I am she, the brunette said, turning to face one of the mirrored panels on the wall.

And she is me, the redhead replied, pulling a small knife from where it had been embedded in her chest.

As the blade was drawn out, both women began to bleed; their wounds identical but for the brunette's right forearm. The mirrored panel began to crack and splinter, sending heavy shards of glass tumbling to the floor.

Then another began to crack.

And another.

Soon, the sound of shattering glass filled the room and he turned his face away from the shrapnel, feeling tiny pricks puncturing his skin.

Madeleine!

He raised a hand to protect his eyes, trying to see through the fog of glass to find her.

She isn't here, the brunette said, her voice rising above the sound of glass panels shattering, their number as infinite as the possibilities within his own imagination.

She'll be joining us, soon, the redhead told him.

No! he shouted, and his body reared up from the bed in his hotel room, his hand connecting with Madeleine's shoulder as she tried to sleep.

She rolled over, unsure of what to do for the best, then tried to take his hand.

But he shook her off, as his body waged a terrible battle on the frontiers of his own mind.

In his dream, a child appeared before him, small and chubby with pigtails in her hair.

Papa?

He shook his head.

Where's your daddy? he asked her, but she ran away from him.

Wait!

He held out a hand to stop her, but the skin of his hand was old and more weathered than before, and, as he turned, he caught sight of himself in the broken slivers of glass still clinging to the wall.

His father.

Alex spun away from the reflection and straight into his mother's steely grip. He tasted blood in his mouth, an old wound he'd suffered as a boy, and he tried to break free of her, once and for all.

But the arms held steadfast, and her voice whispered in his ear.

Blood is thicker than water. Nothing can come between a mother and her son.

"Alex!" Madeleine cried, giving him a firm shake. "Alex, wake up!"

He did, suddenly and completely, and his hands grasped

her slim shoulders as he struggled to acclimatise himself in the real world.

"Sorry," he said, immediately letting go of her arms and checking to see if his hands had left a mark. "Did I hurt you?"

"No, not really," she said. "It came as more of a shock."

"I'm sorry," he said again, feeling horribly exposed. "I don't normally—"

"Share your bed? Yes, I think I can see why."

She put a hand on his chest, feeling the heavy pounding of his heart as it continued to race.

"It must have been a bad one," she said. "Do you want to talk about it?"

Alex shook his head, feeling out of his depth and unsure how to proceed. Few people had ever witnessed his night terrors, and he took good care to keep it that way. He devoted his life to other people's wellbeing, rarely his own, which seemed to be deferred with every new emergency that came along. At Southmoor, he saw the most extreme cases of mental torment, which tended to relegate his own troubles much further down the list of 'necessary action' when he compared them with the plight of those far more in need of urgent attention.

"It's okay to lean on somebody, once in a while," she said.

Alex looked across at her pale body silhouetted in the early morning light and wondered what that might be like. The only person he'd ever confided in was Bill Douglas and, even then, there were some things he'd withheld.

"Thank you," he said. "I'm sorry you were so rudely awakened."

She smiled.

"I'm often up early," she said. "Some of the shoots start before dawn, so we catch the best light and miss the majority of the commuter crowds."

He leaned over to brush her lips with his own, then padded towards the bathroom. Before he could make it that far, he caught his own reflection in the mirror above the dressing table.

Something clicked, like a latch falling neatly into place.

He crossed the room swiftly, keying in the code to open the safe, where he kept the police dossier. Madeleine sat up in the bed and frowned at him.

"What are you doing?"

"What I should have done days ago," he muttered. "The truth has been staring me in the face, all along."

A moment later, he excused himself to make an urgent telephone call, but before he made it as far as the door, he spun around again and caught the pyjama bottoms Madeleine was ready to throw at him.

"Thanks," he mumbled, and her soft laughter followed him into the corridor outside.

CHAPTER 28

The sun had barely risen in the sky by the time Gregory made his way to the 7ᵗʰ Arrondissement and, when Agnés opened the door to him, she wore a look that told him she was severely unimpressed.

"Is it customary to pay house calls at unsociable hours like this in England?"

"You must be joking. Nobody pays house calls in England, after all the government cutbacks," he muttered. "Is Camille awake?"

"Luckily for you, she woke up only a few minutes ago," she said, with another disapproving look in his direction. "That girl needs as much rest as possible, not to be harangued so early in the morning."

"Normally, I'd agree with you," he said. "But this is important, Agnés. I think I may understand the reason for her memory loss."

"I thought it was the attack?"

"Yes and no," he replied. "How has she been this morning?"

"She seems more subdued, today."

He nodded, for it was just as he'd anticipated.

"Agnés, I'd like you to come and join me, please, as a witness."

She looked startled by his choice of words, but was happy to follow him into the living room, where Camille was seated on the sofa nibbling a croissant and watching the changing colours of the sky. "Good morning," he said.

There was a short delay before she turned around.

"Oh, you've come back," she said, brightening up a bit. "I thought you'd forgotten me."

Gregory stepped into the room and gestured towards an empty seat.

"Do you mind if I—?"

"Please, do sit down," she said, politely. "You too, Agnés. Please don't stand around on my account. I feel bad enough, having so many people running after me."

"Sorry to pay such an early visit," he said. "Would you rather I came back later?"

She shook her head.

"It's nice to have some company," she admitted, and then looked immediately apologetic. "Sorry, Agnés, it isn't that I don't enjoy your company, as well."

"*Pas du tout*," the nurse replied.

"Do you remember our chat yesterday?" he asked, and she looked between the pair of them in confusion. "Was that yesterday? I could have sworn it was the day before that you came to visit."

Agnés looked at Gregory, then back to Camille.

"Doctor Gregory came yesterday, don't you remember? You talked about—"

He shook his head, and the nurse fell silent.

"Do you remember why I'm here?"

"To help me," she replied. "Or, try to. Isn't that what you said?"

He smiled.

"I'll certainly do my best," he murmured, and then prepared himself to take a risk. "Do you still want to see yourself, in the mirror?"

She nodded.

"I want to see what the damage is," she replied, calmly. "I need to be able to cope with the stares when I walk down the street."

"I'll take you for that walk later, if you like," Gregory put in.

"A walk? Oh, that would be nice. I feel so—so cooped up in here. It would be good to get out for some fresh air somewhere other than that veranda."

Gregory glanced back towards a tiny iron veranda off the kitchenette, which held a few planters containing various herbs, and nodded.

"First, why don't we take a look at that injury together. Agnés?"

The nurse went off in search of the mirrors she'd locked away, and came back with a smallish, wooden-framed one that usually sat above the bathroom counter. Gregory took it from her and then walked over to where Camille was seated, preparing himself for the unexpected.

"Ready?"

She nodded, and he held out the mirror.

It didn't happen straight away, and Gregory experienced a moment's doubt.

At first, she stared at her pale face with a degree of stoicism that was admirable. With Agnés's help, they peeled back the bandage on her cheek, and she closed her eyes, not wanting to see the puckered stitches running like a train track along one side of her face until she was ready.

When she did pluck up the courage to look, Gregory watched her closely for any shift in mood. And, finally, it came.

While Agnés watched in a kind of awed horror, her patient's face contorted from soft lines, to blind, murderous anger.

"Get away from me," she snarled suddenly, and hit out at the mirror, which would have flown from Gregory's hand, if he hadn't already been anticipating such a response.

Quickly, he handed the mirror back to Agnés, who moved it out of sight.

The woman was crying now, pacing back and forth across the wooden floor.

"Camille?"

"*Don't say that name!*"

"Why not?"

"She's a *killer! A murderer!*"

"Well, it seems you've solved the mystery, *mon ami*," Durand said, cheerfully. "It would have been quite easy for Camille to leave the apartment while her night nurse snored, while maintaining the veneer of an alibi. I'm surprised we didn't think of it, sooner."

"I'm not certain that's what happened," Gregory said. "I can't see what possible reason she would have to kill Juliette."

"She's obviously deranged," the inspector replied. "What reason does she need to have, except madness?"

That was sometimes true, Gregory thought, but he suspected not in the present case. He turned to address the others seated around the conference table at Police Headquarters.

"Camille obviously believes herself to be a killer," he commented. "It doesn't follow that she's right."

"It's enough to bring her in for formal questioning," Segal remarked. "I'd say her admission's as good as a confession."

"I have another theory I want to put forward," Gregory said, before they could begin a witch-hunt.

The Commissaire leaned forward.

"Go ahead, Doctor."

"From the very beginning, we've struggled to make sense of the material facts. In the first place, why would an assailant choose to enter and exit a busy hotel, running the risk of being seen on multiple occasions? For an organised killer who made sure no DNA or other trace evidence was left behind to incriminate him, this seems like a remarkably risky approach to take."

He paused, ticking the next item off his fingers.

"Then, there's the matter of the missing weapon," Gregory continued. "It's true that perpetrators sometimes take their weapons away with them but, in the case of Juliette, her killer left the knife inside her body for us to find. It's a small but important inconsistency, which is common to many first-time killers who panic at the enormity of what they've done."

"But this would be their second time, unless Camille—?" Bernard began to say.

"I'm coming around to Camille, but let us imagine the person who tried to kill her was a rookie, but a smart rookie," he added. "Somebody who knows how evidence works, and what the Technical and Scientific Team would be looking for."

They looked amongst themselves, unsure what to make of it.

"You're implying someone with police training could have killed Juliette?" Durand said, obviously put out.

"Keep an open mind," Gregory murmured. "Turning back to the absence of a weapon, I think it's worth questioning why Camille Duquette had glass fragments in her wound."

"They were transplanted when her assailant smashed her head into the mirrored panel in the bedroom," Segal said.

"That's all well and good, but what about the wounds on her torso and arms? They each contain tiny particles of glass, but those areas didn't come into contact with any blunt force trauma. What if they came about from a shard of glass being used as a weapon?"

"You're saying the killer used some of the broken glass, rather than bringing his own knife? It seems a risky business," Durand said.

"Murder tends to be," Gregory replied. "But, in this case, I don't think it was planned at all."

The others in the room looked amongst themselves.

"What do you mean, Doctor? To achieve the kind of forensically-clean crime scene we've been dealing with, there must have been a degree of planning before the attack."

"What other explanation could there be for the lack of DNA or other trace evidence being found at the crime scene in the Hôtel Violette?" he asked, rhetorically. "My friend, Professor Douglas, told me yesterday that, sometimes, the simplest answer is the correct one and, in this case, I believe he's right. There were no alien DNA samples found at the crime scene because Camille was the only attacker in the room; or, rather, her dual personality was."

The others looked at him as though he'd gone off his merry rocker.

"I've heard it all, now," Segal muttered, with a long-suffering glance towards the Commissaire. "With respect, we have no time for games, Doctor. Now, you expect us to believe that Camille Duquette has a—a, what did you call it?"

"Dual personality," Gregory supplied. "Otherwise known as dissociative identity disorder, characterised by the presence of two or more distinct personality states, accompanied by an inability to recall details beyond what we'd attribute to ordinary forgetfulness. The dissociative amnesia is a facet of this wider disorder but can be diagnosed separately."

"And you believe Camille is one of these 'personality states'?" Durand said. "What about the other one?"

"The 'primary' identity is most likely Camille's original identity, which we know she tried to shake off with Wendy Li's help," Gregory replied. "We won't know the name until she tells us, or we find out through the usual lines of enquiry."

"How can you be sure it isn't something else?" Segal wondered aloud.

Gregory smiled tightly.

"I can't," he said, with a smile. "The problem with dissociative identity disorder is that it's comorbid; it can occur alongside other illnesses and some of the symptoms can appear identical to other syndromes, like post-traumatic stress. DID is a very rare condition, and much-maligned, so it isn't something that I'd automatically suggest. However, in Camille's case, it seems to match the patterns of forgetfulness and shifts in mood she experiences—"

"You mentioned those symptoms being a by-product of her trauma," the Commissaire put in. "What's changed? If Camille herself hasn't introduced another name for the second personality you seem to think exists, why should we be looking for one?"

"It's the only logical explanation," Gregory replied, and thought of a much-beloved quote from Arthur Conan-Doyle, the creator of Sherlock Holmes to illustrate his point. "*Once you eliminate the impossible, whatever remains, no matter how improbable, must be the truth.*"

"We've already investigated the usual channels," Durand agreed. "The Technical and Scientific Team have come back with nothing usable from Camille's hotel room, which either means her attacker was extremely careful, as we first thought, or…"

"There was no attacker at all," Gregory finished for him.

"You can't imagine one 'personality state' attacked the other?" Bernard scoffed. "This is the stuff of fantasy, Commissaire, and a waste of police time."

Caron held up a finger for quiet, and his mouth snapped shut, which was an impressive feat whichever way you looked at it.

"What about her injuries, Doctor? How do you suppose she was able to inflict those cuts herself?"

"Consider the right arm," he replied, and the four other people in the room shuffled their paperwork to find Camille's hospital notes. "There were numerous smaller cuts to her left forearm, indicating she'd used it to defend herself from attack, but there were no lesions to the right forearm, as one might expect—and you can compare it with Juliette's arms, both of which bore the signs of defensive action."

"We already talked about the reasons why there may be no markings on her right forearm," Segal said. "The working theory was that Camille tried to grasp the weapon in her right palm, causing injury to herself."

"And yet, the wound to her palm also contained traces of silicon dioxide, commonly found in glass products," Gregory argued. "Camille is right-handed, but rather than using her right hand to defend herself, my theory is that she used it to attack. However, this isn't a simple case of self-harm, or attempted suicide. To properly understand DID, you need to think of the different personalities as *completely different people*, co-existing in the same body."

"Do they…would they know about each other?" Durand wondered aloud, trying to wrap his head around the concept. "Do they have conversations with each other?"

Gregory shook his head.

"There have been cases in the past where subjects have held conversations, switching between personalities," he replied. "It's…well, it's frankly unnerving, but it's fascinating. It is my belief that the woman's primary identity, whoever she may be, was unaware of the secondary identity, Camille. It's often the case that primary identities are more submissive in nature, more introverted, whereas the 'new' secondary and, sometimes, tertiary identities are more outgoing personalities. In this case, that would seem to tie in with my observations of Camille's behaviour and demeanour, which oscillates between introvert and extrovert, with the full complement of speech and behavioural habits to suit both identities."

"But if the primary identity attacked Camille, the secondary, that seems backward," Durand said, following the logical trail of breadcrumbs. "It would be more likely the other way around."

"You'd think so," Gregory agreed. "But, apparently, Camille did something to anger the primary identity; something so bad, she stepped outside her usual constraints and took it upon herself to attack. Seen from their internal perspective, it would have been terrifying for Camille; as though she was being attacked by a total stranger, or a woman she may only be aware of peripherally. Likewise, the primary identity may have traumatised herself in the process, perhaps believing that she'd killed someone, and the amnesia was a coping mechanism."

"I still don't understand why Camille would claim to have killed someone," Durand said. "In this scenario, it would have been the primary identity who was the aggressor, not Camille."

Gregory nodded.

"After I finish here, and with your permission, I plan to have another, longer session with Camille and her other personality. I may be able to elicit a name and some other details, to try to understand what provoked the attack."

"I think I may be able to help you with that," Durand replied, and all eyes turned to him. "The control room received a contact from one of the doctors at an abortion clinic near Barbès, yesterday afternoon, claiming to recognise the mystery woman we were calling 'Sleeping Beauty'. They say she attended the clinic for a procedure a little under three weeks ago, which must coincide with the time she was discovered by Gabrielle Leroux."

Gregory stood up from his chair and walked over to the window to work off some nervous energy. It took a certain kind of conceptualisation to imagine a body hosting two distinct personalities, who may not like or even know about each other. It was not simply a case of one person displaying different characteristics on alternate days, as he'd first thought. That being the case, the way to think of it was to imagine the primary identity attempting to murder Camille.

"Perhaps the primary identity was unaware that Camille had aborted the foetus, and was devastated when she found out. Seen from her perspective, finding out about the loss of her baby against her will would have been traumatic enough to cause a psychological break, effectively splitting the personalities that may only have been half-formed until then. This would explain the degree of frenzy, and anger, in respect of Camille's injuries, as well as providing an explanation as to why there was no alien DNA found at the scene."

The more he listened, the more Segal was beginning to appreciate the possibilities.

"If you're right, Doctor, this breaks completely new ground," he said, working hard to rein in his excitement. "There's never been another case like it, in the history of the Brigade Criminelle. A woman attacking herself, for having an abortion? It's sensational."

"Aren't you forgetting something?" Caron said, pointedly. "What about Juliette?"

"If Doctor Gregory's theory about Camille is correct, that means we're no longer looking for the same attacker—" Segal said.

"Really? Why not?" Durand put in. "As Doctor Gregory says, you need to think of the primary identity as an aggressor, whatever the provocation might have been. She tried to kill Camille, a woman she believes to be a separate living entity, not understanding that she would have killed herself in the process. Who's to say this primary identity doesn't have a morbid hatred for models, like Camille? Let's not forget, Juliette was also a mother. She may have formed her own view on Juliette's approach to motherhood, fuelled by her own deep sense of loss."

Gregory had to give him credit for catching on quickly.

"Although I'd like to say otherwise, I think the inspector is right; we can't rule out the possibility, especially in the absence of any other suspects."

"That's true enough," Bernard grumbled. "We're getting nowhere fast with Juliette's investigation."

Gregory exchanged a glance with the Commissaire, who gave an almost imperceptible nod, then thought back to his conversation with Madeleine the previous day and wondered whether *le cochon* in the room knew that his days were numbered.

"You never know what's waiting around the corner," he said. "Perhaps there'll be another breakthrough."

CHAPTER 29

When Jean-Pierre Bisset stepped into the foyer of his local Préfecture de Police de Paris in Barbès, he joined the ranks of the disenchanted who waited in line to speak to a bored-looking officer seated behind a reinforced glass cubicle. It was the very last place he wanted to be and, if it wasn't for his errant wife, he'd have avoided it like the plague.

"Theft or assault?" the desk officer said, when Bisset reached the top of the queue some twenty minutes later.

"Neither," he muttered. At least, not today.

"What, then?"

"It's—ah, it's about that woman. The model they're calling 'Sleeping Beauty.'"

"Camille Duquette. What about her?"

Jean-Pierre shuffled his feet, feeling stupid. Really, what were the chances that Eva—his dowdy little wife—had been masquerading as a fashion model?

The more he thought about it, the more ridiculous it seemed.

He muttered his apologies and began to turn away, when something caught his eye. Hanging beside a large, laminated poster touting 'Equal Opportunities and Dignity in the Workplace', was a smaller poster bearing an image of the woman they were calling Camille and a message that read simply, 'DO YOU KNOW THIS WOMAN?'

Yes, he did.

It was his wife, Eva Bisset.

He peered at the poster, studying the lines of her face, and thought it was incredible how different she could look. If he'd known what make-up could do for her…well, he wouldn't have needed to make so many trips to see his favourite girls down in the Quartier Pigalle.

"She's really something, isn't she?"

He dragged his eyes away from the poster and down into the grinning face of the police officer, feeling a sudden and violent urge to wipe the smug grin off his face.

"That's my wife you're talking about," he growled.

To his fury, the man laughed at him from behind the bulletproof glass.

"Sure, she is," he said, looking him up and down. "The woman's lost her memory, not her mind, monsieur."

Incensed, humiliated, Jean-Pierre stormed out of the police station and, a moment later, there came the squeal of tyres as he fired up his delivery van, followed by the customary blare of horns and foul language from his fellow motorists.

But he wasn't listening, all of his attention now fixated on punishing Eva for the embarrassment he'd suffered and the inconvenience of having to fend for himself these past three weeks. She'd gone missing before—sometimes for a few hours, sometimes for a couple of days—and he'd always been careful to remind her of the consequences of her transgression.

Obviously, he'd been far too lenient in the past, because she'd learned nothing at all.

In fact, she'd stayed away even longer, and had insulted his family name by masquerading as somebody she wasn't.

Camille Duquette, he thought, with a sneer.

He parked the van and slammed the door shut behind him with unnecessary force, forcing a smile onto his face as he stepped back inside their café—*his* café, now—and mustered the patience to exchange a word or two with some of the regulars.

"Eh, Jean-Pierre! When is your wife back from her trip?" one old boy called out, as he spooned up a bowl of seafood broth. "Lovely lady. Always gives me an extra bowl."

Does she, indeed?

Jean-Pierre contemplated knocking the old man's teeth down his throat, but instead gave him a pat on the back, for the benefit of anyone who may be watching.

"And I'll do the same," he said, expansively. "Louis! Another bowl for Monsieur Marchant!"

His smile remained fixed in place until he climbed the stairs to the private apartment they kept above the restaurant. Once he'd shut the door behind him, his hands curled into fists. Drunk with anger and adrenaline, he staggered into the master bedroom and looked around at the flowery covers and meagre selection of cheap perfumes she'd left on the dresser below a cheap, framed print of Monet's Garden at Giverny.

He went for the bottles first, scooping them into the bin with a smash of glass, then he made for the single rail of clothes she occupied in the large built-in wardrobe they shared. He caught his own reflection in the mirrored doors and smiled manically before snatching up the jumpers and jeans, the plain tee shirts, and the one beautiful thing she'd ever owned: her mother's wedding dress, which she'd worn on the day he'd told her 'I do'.

He threw it on the bed and looked at it for long minutes.

She needed to be reminded of her duties as a *wife,* and perhaps putting on the old dress while he reminded her would be sufficient to jog her memory. Eva had spent enough time galivanting, earning money that was rightfully *his*, but her time was up. He didn't know who'd attacked her but what did she expect, flaunting herself that way? Maybe it would teach her a lesson in humility, like the one he planned to give her, just as soon as he brought her home.

For better, for worse; until death us do part.

Those were the vows they'd made, and, by God, he'd make sure she kept them.

"Inspector?"

Durand looked up from his desk with a grunt.

"Call from the station in Barbès," one of his team said. "Some bloke's just wandered in, claiming to be Camille Duquette's husband."

"Another one? Tell him to join the queue."

He went back to reading his papers.

"This one might be worth following up. Apparently, he stormed out after the desk officer questioned him, but the officer took a note of the name on the side of his delivery van before he left. He's Jean-Pierre Bisset—runs Café Michel over in Barbès."

"Nice little restaurant," Durand remarked, having enjoyed some falafel from there once. "What makes him so special?"

"The local boys asked around and, apparently, Bisset's wife has a habit of going walkabout, every now and then. She always goes back to him but, word is, she's been gone for almost three weeks, now, and people are starting to ask questions."

Durand looked up at that.

"And his wife's name is?"

"Eva."

Durand fired up his computer and ran a quick search for 'EVA BISSET'.

There was no record in Missing Persons.

"I thought you said she'd gone missing before?"

"Apparently so, but the husband never files a report. The duty officer had never seen the man in the station before."

Durand nodded, ran a separate search for driving license and social security data, and then leaned back in his chair as a grainy passport photo popped onto the screen.

"*Mon Dieu*," he murmured.

The hair was different, the clothes too—and even the way she smiled into the camera told him Eva Bisset was a different personality to Camille Duquette.

And yet they were one and the same.

CHAPTER 30

After the police briefing, Gregory made his way back to Camille's apartment, never more eager to try to piece together the fragments of her broken mind. It had been a battle to keep the procureur away, who'd been eager to see for himself the remarkable case of the woman with two personalities but, as Gregory had told him in no uncertain terms, his patient was not a circus oddity to be gawked at.

In almost all cases of dissociative identity disorder, there was a history of childhood trauma, but significant adult trauma was not unheard of either. To find the root cause, he needed to understand the 'primary identity' and how it had come to split, creating the woman they knew as Camille.

To do that, he needed to keep distractions to a minimum.

He looked across at the woman slumped in the armchair beside the window, every line of her body folded in defeat. She raised a shaking hand to her face, patting the bandage on her cheek and then let it fall away again.

"I haven't heard from the police lately," she said dully. "Do you know whether they've made any progress finding the person who did this?"

Of course, he thought. *The primary identity wouldn't know.*

"Yes, there's been some progress," he said quietly. "But, before we talk about that, can you tell me your name?"

She looked surprised; as if she expected him to know.

"Eva Bisset," she said, casually answering the question that had puzzled them for days.

She became anxious.

"Has Jean-Pierre been in touch? I haven't seen him, and I'm worried he doesn't know where to find me," she said.

"Is Jean-Pierre your husband?"

She nodded, pressing her lips together.

"Would you like me to contact him for you?"

There was a visible battle, the expression on her face shifting until it settled into a sneer.

"Why the hell would I want you to contact *him*? He's nothing but a bully, and he treats her like shit."

"Good morning, Camille," he said, after a pause.

"Hello again," she said, rearranging herself in the chair to get a better look at him. "You look a bit tired, today, Doctor."

"Thanks," he said, with a smile. "You were telling me about Jean-Pierre being a bully. To whom?"

"Her. The woman who works at Café Michel."

"What's her name?" he asked softly.

"Eva."

"What's she like?"

"I don't know...boring, mousy. No good at anything,"

she said, unconsciously repeating the words Jean-Pierre had said, so many times before.

"Have you spoken to her?" he asked.

"I've tried," she said. "But you can't force anyone to leave, can you? It's up to her."

"Have you seen her recently?"

"Not for a while," she said. "I last saw her a few weeks ago, at the café."

"Do you go there regularly?" he wondered.

She shook her head.

"Only a couple of times before," she said. "The day I met Gabrielle Leroux."

"At the Place Vendome?"

"She was there, too. I saw her scooter."

Gregory thought he was beginning to understand the timeline of events. Eva Bisset had been at the Place Vendome making a delivery, when she'd been spotted by Gabrielle Leroux. The meeting triggered a deep desire to be a part of the world she'd only ever seen from afar, but Eva Bisset was in the early stages of pregnancy and knew there was no way in the world her domineering husband would allow her to take up the opportunity.

And so, her psyche created another version of herself who *could*, and named her Camille.

But Camille hadn't wanted the baby.

"Tell me about the abortion, Camille," he said, wondering when or if Eva would return to what was, by any standards, a remarkable conversation.

"How do you know about that?" she asked.

"The clinic got in touch," he said. "They recognised your picture from the news."

"Have I been in the news?"

There was no television in the apartment; only books, lots and lots of them to occupy her mind while she recovered.

"The police put out an appeal to find your family," he explained.

"And has anyone been in touch, yet?"

Rocky ground, he thought.

"Let's talk about that in a moment. You were about to tell me about the abortion, Camille."

She heaved a sigh.

"What do you want to know? I couldn't keep the baby, not with all the campaigns coming up. I didn't even have a place to live."

"Who was the father?" he asked.

Camille frowned at him, her face turning pale.

"Breathe," he said softly. "Take long breaths in and out."

He coached her breathing for a few minutes, pulling her back from a sudden fall in blood pressure that could only have been psychosomatic.

"She said I was a killer," she whispered, staring at the air somewhere above his head. "She—she told me I was just like all the rest of them."

"The rest of who?"

She just shook her head.

"When did she say these things to you, Camille?"

There was a second's pause, and then Eva looked up, no longer the demure, downtrodden housewife, but a mother whose reason for continuing to live had been snatched from her.

"*Don't speak her name to me.*"

The hatred was so strong, so powerful, he could almost feel the force of it pushing him back against the chair.

But he couldn't stop. Not when they were so close to being in the same room, all three of them, together.

"Why? What happened, Eva? Why shouldn't I say her name?"

"She's a murderer," she spat, and her hands crept down to clutch her stomach. "Do you know what she did? What—what she *took* from me?"

More than a foetus, he thought. *Much more than that.*

"You wanted the baby."

"Yes."

Her face crumpled and she bent over, letting out a long, keening wail like a wounded animal. "I'm sorry," he murmured.

He gave it a couple of minutes, and waited while she cried, not holding her hand but comforting her with his quiet presence.

"Tell me about your husband," he said, when the worst had passed.

Eva rested her head on her hand and looked at him with eyes that were twin pools of misery.

"Why—why do you want to know about Jean-Pierre?"

264

"I want to help you but, in order to do that, I need to understand all the elements of your life." *And why you didn't want me to call him.*

"Jean-Pierre is thirty-five," Eva said, proceeding to rattle off the basic facts about the man she'd married. "He's a chef—a brilliant chef," she amended quickly, fearful that he might suddenly burst from the shadows, having heard every word she said. "He runs the restaurant my father started up."

"And you?"

"I help out," she said, downplaying her own contribution.

Her head lifted suddenly, in outrage.

"You do much more than that!" Camille raged. "I've seen you scrubbing floors, balancing books, making deliveries… you never *live*. As for Jean-Pierre, he's a liar and a cheat, and that's the least of his problems."

Anger rippled over Eva's face.

"You don't know anything about my life, or about Jean-Pierre," she snapped.

The woman moved her head this way and that, and Gregory watched in silent fascination as the two women conducted an argument from within the same physical body; her hand gestures changing to suit whichever personality dominated at the time.

"Why don't you show him the scar?" Camille asked. "The one near your eye? Why don't you tell him how *that* happened?"

Eva raised her fingers to the tiny crescent-shaped scar on her right temple, which somehow mattered more than the fresh one running down the length of her face.

"You can tell me how it happened, if you like," Gregory murmured. "I'm here to listen."

Her eyes fell away.

"He didn't mean to do it—"

"Stop it! Stop making excuses for him! He *likes* hurting you, Eva. He wants to destroy whatever confidence you have left."

Eva shook her head, but the tears began to fall again.

"You don't know him like I do," she said. "He's a very passionate person, and he gets carried away."

"Is that what he tells you, Eva?" Gregory asked.

She nodded.

"Really, Doctor, he's a wonderful husband. He tells me he loves me, all the time," she said, and implored him to believe her. "He never means for things to get out of hand, he's just so—so strong…"

"You can't really believe that?" Camille said, in the gentlest tone Gregory had heard, so far. "You can't really be thinking of going back to him—not again?"

Gregory watched their interplay while the tape recorder on his phone captured the exchange, and realised something important. When he'd researched the diagnosis and treatment of dissociative identity disorder, he'd been disheartened to find a general lack of clinical consensus, no systematic, empirically-based approach. There was only a small number of case studies describing the treatments used and, of those, only very few patients achieved a single, unified identity at the end of it all.

He had therefore come to the conclusion that, in order to achieve anything near to unity, the co-habiting personalities must first learn to live together. Accepting and acknowledging the different identities would be the first step in also acknowledging the problem and bringing it out into the light, rather than relying on dissociative amnesia to block out those parts the primary identity didn't want to remember.

And, in the case of Eva and Camille, forgiveness was the key.

CHAPTER 31

Madeleine Paquet left the sheltered housing development where her mother lived with mixed emotions.

On the one hand, her mother was thriving. There was colour in her cheeks, and her mobility seemed to be a little better, after being on the drugs plan for the past couple of years. It was incredible what modern medicine could do.

But it came at a price.

The monthly care bill weighed heavily in her bag, and on her heart. No matter how hard she worked, singing could never pay a bill like that—unless she struck lucky and landed herself a record deal of some kind, which was pie in the sky—leaving no option but to continue as she was.

Trapped.

The modelling was manageable, but she resented having to work for Leroux after all that had happened, and resented having to pretend it was okay. She was, fundamentally, an honest person, who wanted a simple life, with a family and children to love—eventually. There were things she hoped to achieve; things that relied upon her mind, rather than her body. She was tired of speaking without being heard; tired of needing to raise her voice to express an opinion, then being told to be quiet by the men in the room. She was more than the sum total of the shell she lived in.

As she rounded a corner and made her way to her apartment, her thoughts turned to the latest man in her life.

Alexander.

He seemed so unlike all the others she'd known. He listened, for one thing, and seemed to care about her opinion—seeking it out and considering it before choosing whether to agree or disagree. He'd never once belittled her, nor reduced her to an object. The man had principles, but he wasn't afraid to take chances, as he had with her. He had a quiet way about him, an understated strength that she found attractive—but she wasn't blind to the rest.

For all his kindness to them, and his efforts to help them, Alex didn't really *trust* people. He viewed them with suspicion—herself included. She sensed that it wasn't merely the circumstances under which they'd met, or what she'd told him about her past, but rather a default position he occupied, regardless of the company he kept. She wanted to know what had happened to him, what was so *bad* as to fracture his belief, but he held himself apart and whenever she felt she was drawing nearer to the 'real' person, he withdrew even further.

If only Alex would give a little more of himself, or even the hope of more, she might be able to imagine a future with him. As it was, she imagined a life of always trying, always striving, but never quite reaching that elusive goal.

Madeleine let herself into the mansion block where she lived, and set down a small bag of fruit and vegetables while she checked the post box.

At the very top was a plain brown envelope.

Curious, she opened it to find a short stack of photos and, as she glanced at the first few, her stomach began to heave and roll.

Thoughts of being able to support herself and her mother, of ever being able to show her face again, all disappeared into dust; for there, in glossy colour print, were explicit, long-range photographs of her with Alex, alongside older ones taken from some of the parties she'd attended more than two years before.

The very last picture was one of her modelling shots, a nice summer bikini shot of her on a beach, taken the previous summer. It had been defaced with a black marker pen, and a long scar had been added to her face, as well as several more on her torso.

Oblivious to the shock Madeleine had just received, Alex Gregory continued to guide Eva and Camille towards a mutual understanding. On one hand, he was dealing with a downtrodden victim of domestic abuse, whose confidence and perspective had been lost. On the other, he had a confident, unapologetic woman who wanted to waste no more time before grasping everything life had to offer.

Throw a lost baby and some physical trauma into the mix, and there was quite a range of issues to deal with.

The fact both women occupied the same body seemed incidental, by comparison.

"You can't go back to Jean-Pierre," Camille was telling her alter-ego. "You deserve better."

"He loves me," Eva mumbled.

"Do you love *him*?" Camille demanded. "Because, if you do, you're an idiot. Anyone can see he's been screwing around, aside from all the kicks and slaps."

Eva stood up suddenly and began to pace, shaking her head vehemently from side to side while Gregory inched forward in his seat, ready to intervene if necessary.

"He wouldn't do that," she said. "He's—he might have made a lot of mistakes, in the past, but Jean-Pierre wouldn't do that."

"Oh, for goodness' sake, wake up!" Camille shouted. "Why do you think he stays out so late at night? Why do you think he hardly noticed when *you* weren't home, Eva? Because he wasn't there, either."

"Everything would have been different, once the baby came along," Eva cried back. "You took that from me! You took the only thing I had!"

Eva dissolved into pitiful tears, and Gregory held up a hand to prevent Agnés from rushing forward to comfort her. He might have wanted to do the same but, in this conversation between Eva and Camille, they were merely the facilitators. If any kind of resolution was to be reached, the two women must build their own bridge.

"I'm sorry, Eva," Camille said, very quietly. "But I'd do the same again. You think it was just because of the modelling, but it wasn't. Bringing Jean-Pierre's child into the world wouldn't 'fix' him or make him any kinder. It would give him another person to bully, and I couldn't allow that to happen. I had to be strong, for both of us."

In the corner of the room, Agnés put a hand to her mouth to stifle sudden tears and quietly stepped outside. Gregory bore down against his own emotions, hearing the heartache and the sorrow, and he knew they were getting closer.

"I wouldn't have let him hurt the child," Eva whispered. "I'd have killed him, first."

But she thought of all the savage ways Jean-Pierre had wounded her, in body and in mind, and knew that some things were like a tidal wave and simply could not be stopped.

"I'm sorry I attacked you," Eva said, and Gregory realised she was staring at her own reflection in the window, which was like a mirror in the gathering dusk outside. "I'm sorry you were afraid."

Camille nodded.

"What do we do now?" she asked. "I won't be leaving, and neither will you, unless something changes."

"Where would we go? He has all the money—"

"We get a lawyer," Camille said. "A good one. I have some earnings due to me from the shoots I did before—well, before the accident."

Eva nodded.

"Would you come with me?" she asked. "To speak to the police, and to the lawyer?"

"I'll stay with you as long as you need me to," Camille replied, and put her hand out to touch the glass. "We'll work this out, together."

Gregory found himself deeply moved; not by the experience of having witnessed an extraordinary episode in the psychiatric world, but by the power of mutual empowerment. It had not been he, the clinician, who had helped them to understand one another. Eva and Camille had managed that all on their own.

CHAPTER 32

When Gregory returned to his hotel, he found Madeleine waiting for him in the foyer.

She stood up as soon as he entered, and one look at her pale face told him something dreadful had happened.

He covered the distance quickly.

"What's wrong?" he asked, and held her arms in a light grip, for support. "Is it your mother?"

She shook her head.

"No, it's—can we…"

He curved an arm around her shoulders and led her swiftly towards the lift, then up to his bedroom and away from prying eyes. Once they were inside, she sank onto the edge of his bed and pulled an envelope from her handbag.

"This was delivered to me, sometime this morning or last night," she said, holding it out to him. "See for yourself."

He handed her a glass of water, which she held between her numb fingers, while he took the envelope from her and held it on the extreme edge. Having spent long enough in the company of police to know that trace evidence should be preserved, he took a napkin from the minibar and pinched it between his fingers, using it to handle the photos which fell from the envelope and onto the desk.

Gregory was silent as he looked through the paltry collection, his anger rising with every fresh intrusion of their privacy, a feeling that only increased when he turned to the older images of a young woman who had been coerced into a scenario that was now being used against her.

"There was a note," she said.

He saw it, a single sheet of white A4 paper with some printed words on the front. He read its contents, which warned Madeleine of the consequences of speaking out, specifically that the images would be handed over to every press outlet in Paris and that her career and, perhaps more importantly, her reputation would be destroyed.

"I'm not ashamed of the images of the two of us, although I doubt the Police Judiciaire will feel that way," she said, in a voice heavy with tears. "It's the older images, they're…" She swallowed bile. "It's like a living reminder of everything I've tried to forget and move past. I don't remember anyone taking photographs but, obviously, they did. I can't—Alex, I can't begin to imagine how much this will hurt my mother."

Her voice broke and he moved to sit beside her on the bed, pulling her into his arms and wrapping them tightly around her.

"It doesn't have to hurt her," he said quietly. "Madeleine, these images, and the person or people who sent them, only have any power so long as we're afraid. We need to regain the upper hand, and neutralise the threat."

"What do you mean?"

"The person who delivered this to you has been very stupid," he said. "Hand-delivered items are the easiest to trace back, and that's discounting any CCTV that might have captured them pushing it through your letterbox. There's only one thing to do, and that's take it to the police."

"But *le cochon* must be one of them," she said. "How do we know who to tell?"

"We have to trust someone," he said, and she looked up at him with a startled expression. "We'll go first thing tomorrow morning. It's the right thing to do."

"But Alex, they'll probably kick you off the case," she said. "I don't want your professional reputation to be damaged—"

"So you would sacrifice your own, instead?" he asked, and shook his head. "No, Madeleine. We knew that, by continuing to see one another, we were trespassing over a professional boundary. I'll accept the consequences of my decision."

"I'll have to tell them all about what happened," she said, half to herself.

"Do you think you can do it?" he asked, with a hint of challenge that wasn't lost on her.

"Yes," she said. "I can do it."

He took her hand.

"We'll do it together," he said, echoing Camille's words, only an hour before.

"You stupid old man."

Gabrielle Leroux looked at her husband with eyes that were narrowed in contempt.

"My love, I didn't think—"

Her soft, pale hand connected with the side of his face in a hard *slap*.

"I'll do the thinking, in future."

She paced away to pour herself a stiff drink, which she knocked back in one gulp before placing both palms on the marble countertop of their enormous kitchen.

"It was idiotic to deliver that envelope," she said, feeling Armand hovering beside her, desperate once again for her approval. "Even *le cochon* won't be able to save us, now."

"Maybe—"

"Quiet," she snarled, turning to him with eyes that were like cold chips of ice. "This isn't the eighties, anymore. Things are different. Do you think I didn't know about your little parties? Do you think I'm blind?"

"I—"

"Shut up. I tolerate it for the good of the business, for the good of the *brand*. At least have the decency to try to hide your exploits, in future."

"There won't be—"

She simply shook her head.

"The priority is to keep you out of prison, and out of the papers. I don't care what it takes. You need to go to Caron."

"The Commissaire? No, she isn't part of it—"

"I know," Gabrielle said, and rolled her eyes heavenward. "You will go to her first thing in the morning, and explain that you will turn on *le cochon* so long as you are afforded immunity from prosecution and your name is kept off the official papers."

"Do you think it will work? It needs to be very discreet…"

Gabrielle turned to him and pinned him with a glare.

"You will make *sure* it works, Armand—otherwise you're finished."

"We—"

"Oh, no," she interrupted, in that breathy voice he'd once found alluring. "Not 'we', Armand. *You.* Perhaps you're forgetting that I have independent means, whereas you've spent the past twenty years pissing away everything you ever made on the stock market. My father will have no desire to bankroll you any further, and I will simply divorce you and tell my tale as another one of your hapless victims, whilst taking my money and my brand with me."

He thought he might embarrass himself by crying.

"Please, Gaby. It was a stupid mistake."

"First thing tomorrow morning," she repeated, before stalking out of the room.

CHAPTER 33

Monday 30th September

The leaves fell in shades of brown and gold, lining the avenues of Paris as the city recovered from a week of parties, shows and press junkets—and, of course, the murder of one of its most high-profile models. The press continued to report on Juliette Deschamps' murder, alongside Camille Duquette's mysterious identity crisis, and the women's movement with the slogan 'JE SUIS ELLE, ET ELLE EST MOI' had seized on their experiences as prime examples of a toxic patriarchy, not merely within the fashion world, but throughout their beautiful city.

And they were about to add another face to their number.

Madeleine Paquet leaned on Gregory's arm for support as they arrived outside a smart front door in the Marais district, not far from his hotel on the other side of the Seine. It was one of the oldest parts of the city, home to the legendary Bastille and now an upmarket residential and shopping area, popular with tourists and locals alike.

"It'll be fine," he murmured, giving her hand a quick squeeze. "Just tell the truth."

Commissaire Caron opened the door herself.

"Thank you for agreeing to meet with us away from the Trente-Six," Gregory said, once they were seated around her kitchen table.

"You told me very little over the phone," Caron said. "But the fact we're speaking here and not at the PJ tells me it concerns my department."

Gregory nodded.

"Allow me to introduce Madeleine Paquet," he said, shifting towards the woman seated beside him. "You may recognise her name from the file."

Caron nodded.

"As well as the moisturising cream I use every morning," she said, with a smile that was designed to put the woman at her ease. "What is it you'd like to tell me?"

Madeleine pulled out the envelope, and allowed its contents to do the talking.

Caron exchanged a glance with both of them, before pulling on a pair of gloves and picking up the unassuming bits of paper.

When she'd finished, she stacked the photographs and returned them to the envelope before peeling off the gloves again, and steepling her fingers against her chin.

"Setting aside the obvious conflict of interest that is brought about by the relationship between you, let's address the bigger picture, first. Do you know who sent this to you?"

Madeleine proceeded to explain her history with Maison Leroux, and in particular its owner, Armand, who was in the habit of coercing new, up-and-coming models like herself to attend parties he held routinely for important people in the city and beyond.

"How important?" Caron asked, with a sinking heart.

"I don't remember all of them," Madeleine replied, but went on to name several senior figures whose names she recognised.

By the time she'd finished, Caron was incensed. She knew what it was to fight and claw her way up the ladder, and what it took to stay there. At least half of the people Madeleine had just named had, at one time or another, offered to help with her departmental budget at the next council meeting. But there were lines in the sand, invisible ones she refused to cross—not even for her own self-interest. She kept a tidy house and, if there was a clean-up operation to do at the Trente-Six, she didn't mind getting her hands dirty.

"This person—*le cochon*—do you know who it is?"

Madeleine shook her head.

"Never mind. You did the right thing bringing this to my door, and I'll mount an enquiry using our own internal affairs officers. Would you be willing to make a statement?" she asked.

Madeleine glanced at Gregory, who gave her hand another encouraging squeeze.

"Yes," she said. "I'll go on the record."

Caron nodded, understanding the commitment that took, and what the woman stood to lose.

"If your lawyer files a private civil claim, as well as the criminal complaint, you can sue Armand Leroux and any associated persons for damages," she pointed out. "That might help with your mother's care, down the road, if anything should affect your main source of income."

Madeleine thanked her, and Gregory waited patiently while they completed the necessary forms and paperwork.

"Well done," Caron said, when the worst was over. "That can't have been easy, but I applaud you for your bravery. You can be assured I'll handle this with the utmost care."

"It's—Alex helped me to overcome the worst," Madeleine said, trying to mitigate the force of the hammer that was about to fall in his direction. "He helped me to find the courage and the self-esteem to come forward."

Caron turned her attention to her other visitor.

"I'm glad your relationship has had such a positive impact," she said, quietly—and acknowledged that, in coming there, he too had taken a big risk.

"You must have known that embarking upon a personal relationship with a witness in the case of Camille Duquette was ill-advised," she said, severely.

Gregory gave a short nod.

"I did."

"And you chose to do it anyway," she marvelled. "May I ask why—or is the answer very much obvious?"

Gregory turned to look at Madeleine, and he shook his head slowly.

"There's nothing obvious about Madeleine," he said

softly, and watched tears prick the corners of her eyes. "She's a talented, intelligent and interesting woman, and I was bowled over the first time I met her. I'll never regret the time we spent together, not even if it costs me my professional reputation."

Caron heard the 'goodbye' that was implicit in the words he had spoken and, by the look of her, Madeleine had heard it, too.

"It's the same for me," she managed, reining in her emotions with a fierceness she would later feel proud of.

"Well," Caron said, briskly. "The question is, what to do about it? On the one hand, you are fully aware of your actions, and I would be within my rights to contact your employer at Southmoor Hospital to inform them of the transgression."

Gregory lifted his chin, preparing himself for the worst. His work was everything to him, his life and soul—it represented years of training and clinical work, thousands of patients he had helped, to the best of his ability, and some he couldn't. If it was taken away from him, he could hardly imagine what he would do instead.

"On the other hand," Caron continued. "Your services as a profiler and in a clinical capacity have been invaluable to us. Thanks to your insight and work with her, Camille Duquette—or Eva Bisset—is no longer a mystery to us. Her progress has been exponential and, with the assistance of a local psychiatric team, she can build on her newfound strength and carve out a new life for herself, if she wishes."

"What about Juliette's murder?" Madeleine asked.

"That's another area for which I must thank you," she admitted. "Following your telephone call yesterday morning, I took your advice and ordered an express service on the DNA samples taken from Juliette's apartment."

Gregory leaned forward, anxious to hear the news.

"And?"

"It's as you thought," she said. "I've also ordered covert surveillance of Camille's apartment, as you suggested."

"But—I thought that *le cochon* had killed Juliette?" Madeleine said, in confusion. "I thought they wanted to silence her, or something of that kind?"

Gregory shook his head.

"The coercion, blackmail and sexual assault you and Juliette suffered is separate," he told her. "We believe Juliette's killer had another motive. Following Camille's attack, when the police thought that a third party was responsible, this perpetrator took the opportunity to kill Juliette and hoped that the crime would be attributed to the same person."

"But Camille attacked herself—or rather, Eva did," Caron said. "That must have been a crushing moment for Juliette's killer, because they could no longer rely upon some mystery assailant as a scapegoat. The only person left to try to pin it on is Camille."

"Eva," Gregory corrected, with a smile. "They want the police to believe that, if she's crazy enough to try to kill her alter-ego in a frenzied attack, she'd be crazy enough to kill her friend."

"You can't let that happen," Madeleine said.

"I won't," Caron assured her. "This one may be a different breed, but it's just another kind of pig."

It was mid-morning by the time Commissaire Caron returned to her office, where her assistant informed her that a visitor and his lawyer had been waiting since the building first opened.

"Well, naturally, send them through," she said, and placed a bet with herself about who it would be.

And won.

"Good morning, Monsieur Leroux, what a pleasant surprise," she said, and nodded to the wily-looking solicitor who skulked in afterwards. "Won't you sit down?"

Leroux had spent much of the morning sweating through his shirt, creating a meaty aroma which wafted into the office with him, and her nose wrinkled.

"Coffee? Tea?"

"No—nothing, thank you," he stuttered. "I, um, I was hoping to have a word—"

"My client, Armand Leroux, is in possession of valuable information that may benefit the Police Judiciaire. In particular, the corrupt activities of Felix Bernard—also known as *le cochon*—who over the course of many years…"

Caron listened while terms and exchanges were laid out, and made the appropriate sounds of surprise and disapproval as the monologue went on. All the while, she thought of women younger than herself, and older, who were subjected to the kind of selfish acts committed by the balding, overweight man seated in front of her, and wondered how often their small acts of courage and defiance were defeated behind closed doors.

Not this time.

"I agree to provide you with immunity from prosecution as regards any complaints or charges yet to be filed. I assume you're not aware of any that are presently underway?" she asked, with a bland expression.

"None at all, ma'am," the solicitor replied, confidently.

"In that case, let me call in my colleague to begin the paperwork, and you can make your statement."

A few minutes later, she watched Armand Leroux head off to give his statement with a spring in his step, no doubt congratulating himself on having averted a very near miss. She waited until his lumbering figure was out of sight, then smiled to herself.

She happened to know that Madeleine Paquet's criminal complaint had been filed an hour earlier, and the papers were due to be served at Armand's home address that afternoon, unless they had already been delivered.

With any luck, it would hit the news in time for the press conference she'd arranged with Madeleine Paquet for later that day.

CHAPTER 34

"You still look like ass, my friend."

Durand looked across at Gregory from the driver's seat of his Citröen, then back at the road ahead.

"I heard about Bernard and Leroux," he continued. "I wish it came as a surprise."

Gregory nodded.

"Sometimes, the simplest answer is the right one," he said, reiterating Bill Douglas's advice to him a couple of days before.

"I'll be sorry to see you go," Durand said. "You're sure you can't stay on a few more days? Come and have dinner with Sandrine and me, one more time."

Gregory smiled his thanks.

"Please thank her for the invitation, but it's time I returned to my own work, and my own life."

"I thought, maybe for a while, that there might be another reason for you to stay," Durand offered, with a meaningful wiggle of his eyebrows. "Madeleine is a lovely woman."

"She is," Gregory acknowledged. *And she deserves a lovely man.* "I can't give her what she wants, at the moment. It would be unfair to stay any longer."

Durand let out a small sigh, and shook his head. Gregory thought he heard him mutter something about the folly of youth.

"Which train are you getting?" he asked, as the Gare du Nord came into view up ahead.

"Whichever one comes first," Gregory replied.

The car swung onto a side street and the inspector parked on the kerb, narrowly missing a street vendor, before turning to face Gregory with a serious, fatherly expression.

"I want to say, what you did for Camille—for Eva," Durand corrected. "It was like magic."

Gregory shook his head.

"They did it themselves," he replied. "I've left the names of several reputable psychiatrists in the area, any of whom would be equipped to take her case forward and oversee her recovery in the long term."

"That's good of you," Durand nodded. "And I understand Gabrielle Leroux has agreed to finance her apartment for the remainder of the year."

"Trying to mitigate the PR damage?" Gregory wondered, and Durand tapped his bulbous nose.

"You said it."

"Well, this is me," Gregory said, and held out a hand, but found himself engulfed in a bear hug instead.

"Don't be a stranger," Durand said, giving him one of his special manly slaps on the back.

"Au revoir," Gregory said, and raised a hand in farewell as he made his way to the entrance, chuckling as he heard the toot of horns as Durand pulled away behind him.

Jean-Pierre Bisset checked the address he had been given and brought his delivery van to a standstill near to the building where Eva was staying.

He looked around the smart mansion blocks and sneered.

Bitch. Living like this, while I slave over a stove all day.

He made his way along the pavement and stood for a moment watching the entrance, which had an intercom system.

Shit.

He looked up and down the pavement on either side, and spotted a woman making her way towards him with two large shopping bags. He didn't know where she was headed but, as it happened, his luck was in, and she paused beside the front door to hunt for her key.

He moved like lightning.

"Let me help you with those," he said, and gave her one of his best smiles. "I'm just heading inside, myself."

"Oh, who are you here to see?"

"The lady on the first floor," he replied, holding the bags solicitously while she found her key. "I can't tell you her name, because she doesn't want anybody to know she's here."

"Ah, I think I know the one," she said, conspiratorially. "I've seen people going in and out, police too. Well, you tell her from me, I hope she gets better very soon."

"Oh, I will," he promised, and followed her inside.

Durand was whistling by the time he arrived at Eva and Camille's apartment, but he stopped and slowed his car as he caught sight of a man running across the street to her building, where he seemed to exchange a word with an elderly woman, before gaining entry.

Jean-Pierre Bisset?

He'd seen the man's criminal record, and it didn't make for light reading.

Quickly, he reached for his radio to call it in, but then let it fall away again as he spotted three covert surveillance officers closing in from unmarked police cars dotted around the street. He frowned, wondering why he hadn't been informed, and then the truth hit him like a thunderbolt.

They knew.

They knew, and they'd been waiting for *him* to arrive.

He thought of the kit he'd stashed in the boot of his car—everything he'd planned to use after dark to gain access to the apartment and stage Eva's suicide—and realised he'd need to dispose of it as soon as possible. After that, everything he had, everything that mattered, was at home with Sandrine.

With a grind of gears, he swung out in a U-turn and sped off in the direction of La Chapelle, leaving the stench of burning tyres in his wake.

———

Eva was reading about the process of instigating divorce proceedings in Paris, relying upon Camille to offer helpful explanations or advice, when there came a knock at the door.

"*J'arrive!*" Agnés called out, and hurried to the door, expecting to find Gregory on the doorstep.

But she had barely reached for the handle when it splintered and swung open beneath the forceful boot of the man who stood outside.

"I'm here for my wife," he said.

"No! No, monsieur!"

Agnés tried to block him with her body but, with an angry growl, he sent her sprawling with a hard, back-handed hit.

Eva heard his voice and began to tremble violently, her body otherwise frozen and immobile.

"Move! Come on!" Camille shouted, and began to get up, only to fall to the floor again and huddle shivering beside the window.

"I can't—can't—he'll kill us both."

"He'll kill us both anyway," Camille whispered. "He's out of control, Eva. He won't stop. He's hurt Agnés."

Eva heard the crash of the nurse falling to the floor trying to defend her, and something began to rise up. Her fingers curled around the edge of the sofa and she found the strength to drag herself into a crouching position, her eyes darting around the room to seek out a weapon.

"The vase," Camille whispered. "The vase, on the coffee table."

It held the flowers Madeleine had brought her the previous day, and she grasped the edge of it as Jean-Pierre entered the room, his eyes black with anger.

"Time to go home," he said, very softly. "You've been a very, *very* bad wife, Eva."

Her body shaking, Eva managed to stand, drawing herself up to her full height to face him across the width of the coffee table.

"What have you got there, my love? Are you planning to hit me with that, eh?"

He laughed at her, prowling around the edge of the table like a panther stalking its prey.

"Come on, then, if you think you can. Hit me, Eva. Hit me with that vase."

He was within striking distance now, and her pupils were dilated with terror.

"Dear God, you look even worse than I imagined," he said.

Her hand shook, but she gripped the vase tighter.

"You're coming home, where you belong," he said again. "This is the last time you humiliate me, like this—"

He grasped her free arm and twisted it painfully, so hard she feared it might break.

"Do it," Camille whispered. "Do it now."

With a sharp cry, Eva brought the vase crashing down upon his head at precisely the same moment the police burst through the front door.

Jean-Pierre staggered, then fell to his knees, a small cut bleeding from the top of his head. She knew from the look in his eyes that, if they'd been alone, he wouldn't have stopped. She'd disabled him, but not stopped him, because a beast like him would never stop until the final act.

"I'll be seeing you again," he promised her, as he was dragged away by officers in plain clothes. "You're nothing without me. *Nothing*!"

Eva and Camille watched him leave, and then hurried to help the nurse who lay semi-concussed on the hallway floor. A police officer was already tending to her, and tried to help them too.

"No, no, don't worry about me. Take care of Agnés."

"It'll be alright, *petite*," the nurse said, and grasped the hand that was offered.

CHAPTER 35

The sun was high in the sky by the time Inspector Durand pulled up outside the apartment he had shared with his wife and two children for almost thirty years. He didn't know what he could do; whether he could appeal to Sandrine that he'd been falsely accused—perhaps she'd accept it was a case of mistaken identity. His brain worked like lightning to formulate a believable lie to tell his wife, but not once did the question of Juliette, or Anais, cross his mind.

He dropped his key at the front door and swore, finally managing to get the offensive bit of metal into the slot before hurrying inside.

But he was not alone.

Sandrine was seated in her usual spot on the sofa, staring at the door with eyes that burned a hole straight into his very soul.

"Sandie," he said, and then watched in horror as Gregory stepped out of the kitchen, with Caron in tow.

He turned, to retreat back the way he had come, but saw the flashing lights of a squad car through the single pane of glass in the front door and knew that he'd come to the end of the road.

"How did you find out?" he whispered.

Gregory looked at him with an unreadable expression.

"It was your reaction to the little girl that first made me wonder," Gregory replied, and then walked across to the wall, where, amongst the multitude of framed photographs cataloguing a lifetime, there was a photograph taken from his daughter's school showing all the children graduating that year.

Amongst them was Juliette Deschamps.

Gregory plucked it from the wall and held it out, for all to see.

"Elodie and Juliette used to spend time together," Sandrine said, raggedly. "The girls would stay here, or go out together. You used to give her a lift home."

She looked up at her husband, the father of her children, and felt sick with grief.

"That's coincidence," he said, tremulously. "So my daughter went to school with Juliette? Does that make me a killer?"

"No," Caron said. "But the DNA evidence we have against you is irrefutable."

"There's no DNA evidence," Durand said, confidently. *He'd made sure of it.*

"Not on Juliette, perhaps," Caron agreed. "But you should know, Mathis, given all your years of experience, that during the process of their investigation the Technical and Scientific

Team take samples from the victim's family in order to eliminate their DNA from the list of alien or suspect DNA."

His stomach performed a slow flip, and he closed his eyes, because he knew what they had done and what they had found.

"Anais's DNA was part of that process," Caron said. "And do you know what we found, Mathis? Fifty per cent of her DNA matches yours, and there's only one possible explanation for that."

Durand passed weary hands over his face, then looked at the mottled skin, remembering how he'd scrubbed at them, to remove the tarnish of murder.

"I'm sorry," he told his wife. "She was asking for money, and threatening to tell you…"

Sandrine rose from the sofa and looked him dead in the eye.

"I would have been hurt, and heartbroken by your deception, but I would have welcomed Juliette and her daughter into this family. Now…what you've done…"

She shook her head, in disgust.

"I can hardly stand to look at you."

Later that afternoon, Gregory watched the press conference from the departures lounge at the Eurostar terminal at the Gare du Nord. He listened to Madeleine make a bold, brave speech about her ordeal, and smiled at the brief eulogy she gave for her friend, Juliette. But it was the final words she spoke that resonated with him the most and gave him something he scarcely had to spare.

Hope.

"In a world where women are dying or being driven to extreme mental health conditions at the hands of powerful men in this community and around the world, I hope that we can learn one thing and remember it in times of sadness such as this. Whether you happen to be a man or a woman, or identify as neither, *I am she, and she is me.* We are only as good as the world we create around us and I, for one, believe we can do better—for our sons and for our daughters."

As the press clamoured to throw questions about her dealings with Maison Leroux, Gregory spotted a little redheaded girl in the arms of her grandmother, standing to the side of the platform.

"Bonne chance," he said, before hitching a holdall over his shoulder and making his way to the platform.

It was time to go.

Alex Gregory will return in—

BEDLAM

In a world gone mad, who can you trust?

Fresh from a high-profile case in the Paris fashion world, elite forensic psychiatrist and criminal profiler Dr Alexander Gregory receives a call from the New York State Homicide Squad. The girlfriend of a notorious criminal has been admitted to a private psychiatric hospital and can no longer testify in his upcoming trial. Without her, their case will collapse but, amidst reports that the staff are as unpredictable as their patients, who can the police trust?

In desperation, they turn to an outsider and now Gregory must find the courage to step inside the fortified walls of Buchanan Hospital to uncover the truth. The question is, will he ever be the same again?

Murder and mystery are peppered with dark humour in this fast-paced thriller set amidst the spectacular Catskill Forest.

Don't miss book #3 of the Alexander Gregory Thrillers—available in February 2020!

If you would like to be kept up to date with new releases from LJ Ross, please complete an e-mail contact form on her Facebook page or website, **www.ljrossauthor.com**

ABOUT THE AUTHOR

LJ Ross is an international bestselling author, best known for creating atmospheric mystery and thriller novels, including the DCI Ryan series of Northumbrian murder mysteries which have sold over four million copies worldwide.

Her debut, *Holy Island*, was released in January 2015 and reached number one in the UK and Australian charts. Since then, she has released a further fifteen novels, all of which have been top three global bestsellers and thirteen of which have been UK #1 bestsellers. Louise has garnered an army of loyal readers through her storytelling and, thanks to them, several of her books reached the coveted spot whilst only available to pre-order ahead of release.

Louise was born in Northumberland, England. She studied undergraduate and postgraduate Law at King's College, University of London and then abroad in Paris and Florence. She spent much of her working life in London, where she was a lawyer for a number of years until taking the decision to change career and pursue her dream to write. Now, she writes full time and lives with her husband and son in Northumberland. She enjoys reading all manner of books, travelling and spending time with family and friends.

If you enjoyed *Hysteria*, please consider leaving a review online.

If you would like to be kept up to date with new releases from LJ Ross, please complete an e-mail contact form on her Facebook page or website, **www.ljrossauthor.com**

If you enjoyed *Hysteria*, why not try the bestselling DCI Ryan Mysteries by LJ Ross?

HOLY ISLAND

A DCI RYAN MYSTERY (Book #1)

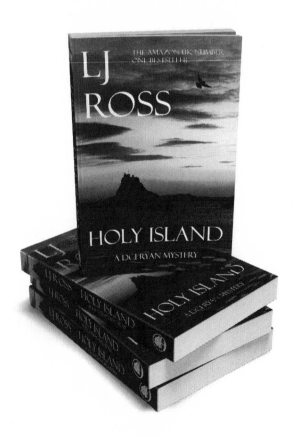

Detective Chief Inspector Ryan retreats to Holy Island seeking sanctuary when he is forced to take sabbatical leave from his duties as a homicide detective. A few days before Christmas, his peace is shattered, and he is thrust back into the murky world of murder when a young woman is found dead amongst the ancient ruins of the nearby Priory.

When former local girl Dr Anna Taylor arrives back on the island as a police consultant, old memories swim to the surface making her confront her difficult past. She and Ryan struggle to work together to hunt a killer who hides in plain sight, while pagan ritual and small-town politics muddy the waters of their investigation.

Murder and mystery are peppered with a sprinkling of romance and humour in this fast-paced crime whodunnit set on the spectacular Northumbrian island of Lindisfarne, cut off from the English mainland by a tidal causeway.